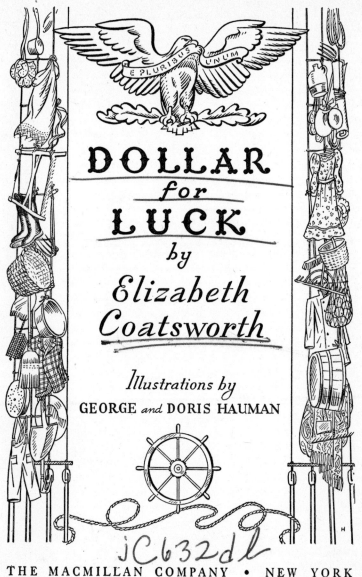

DOLLAR
for
LUCK
by
Elizabeth Coatsworth

Illustrations by
GEORGE *and* DORIS HAUMAN

THE MACMILLAN COMPANY • NEW YORK

For Mary Wambaugh
the best of friends and neighbors

Chapter One

EVERYONE knew her patched sails and burdened shrouds and the faded paint of the eagle at her bow.

"There's the store boat!" Mr. Philbrook called in at the kitchen door to Mrs. Philbrook, who was washing the breakfast dishes. She looked out of the window and smiled.

"I'm almost out of thread," she exclaimed. "Think I'll leave the plates to drain and get right down to the wharf."

"You'd best," said Mr. Philbrook. "But thread! Thread will only be the beginning."

He took a thin wallet out of the pocket of the vest he wore over his shirt and counted out three rumpled dollar bills and handed them to his wife. "Half a mind to go with you, but I've a pile of work waiting for me down at the shop."

She was already untying her apron and patting

[1]

her hair smooth at the little mirror beside the back door.

"Like to change my dress, but haven't time. Maybe the boys'd want to go with me." She was already half up the path to the street and never lost a step as she shouted:

"Ra-alph!

"Stu-art!

"Ken-*neth!*"

A shout answered her from the door of the boat shop down by the water, and the two big boys appeared on the threshold, their natural blondness added to by a sprinkling of sawdust.

"Store boat's in!" shouted Mrs. Philbrook as she started down the road. "Want to come?"

"Too busy now," Ralph shouted back. "Have a good time, Ma."

"Where's Ken?" This was over her shoulder.

"Prob'ly down at the wharf ahead of you," Mr. Philbrook called after her, but by this time Ella Small had appeared from the next house and the two women were hurrying down the road, side by side, talking as they went, while Mrs. Timothy Bent and elderly Mr. Young came racing down their separate walks, the screen doors banging behind them.

Half the village of Friendship was waiting for

the old schooner as she edged in between two fishing boats to make fast at the wharf. There was a man aboard and a woman, wearing a short skirt over a pair of breeches and rubber boots, and a dark little girl at the wheel, bringing the vessel in as slick as a gull catching a fish head.

Everyone knew Cliff and Belle Trask, but the girl was new. What was her name and where did she come from? They were sizing her up. Eleven or twelve perhaps, a little too thin, but pretty if she hadn't looked so gloomy. Knew how to handle the old *Pluribus Unum* anyhow.

Most people left out the "E" of the *E Pluribus Unum* which was written on the scroll coming out of the eagle's beak at the bow, just like the legend on the silver 1872 dollar for which the schooner had been named and which was still nailed to the mast after twenty years. The old *Pluribus* took handling, being cranky by nature and so obscured by the brooms and pots and pans and hoes and shovels and potato baskets hauled up on her shrouds that some people called her the Sailing Hatrack. Not that she always wore her gear that way, only on pleasant days when coming into port, but the banging of dishpans in the wind and the thump of hoes or shovels against each other and the creak of cordage and old blocks made music for the store boat as she sailed grandly to her station.

The first person aboard was Ken Philbrook, who went over the side like a yellow-haired monkey while the schooner was still three feet from the wharf. Ken wasn't interested in buying. He was just mad over any, and every, kind of vessel.

"Hello, Cliff," he called to the master. "Hello, Belle! Want me to help run out the gangplank?"

They had already dropped the sails; the furling could come later. As the women poured over the side in a flood of eagerness, making for the cabin where most of the dry goods from Boston were stored, anxious to choose a dress pattern or a bonnet before the prettiest ones had been taken, Ken retreated to the wheel where the girl still stood.

"What's your name?"

[4]

She looked as though she wouldn't answer and then said briefly, "Emily."

"Mine's Ken. Kenneth Philbrook. What's the rest of your name?"

She looked away.

"None of your business!" she said at last.

Ken didn't press the question.

"My dad builds sloops over there—that's his boat shop down under the white house with the lilacs you see, just beyond Josiah Bent's fish house further out. Dad used to go fishing, but one time he started to build him a new sloop and she looked so good Tom Southwick came along and bought her and before he got the next one built Alonzo Durgin bought *her* and it's been like that ever since. Dad's never had time to build one for himself."

"Should think you'd be glad," the girl answered, looking towards Ken's house rather than the boat shop. "Your ma's got some pretty flowers."

"And don't I get tired weeding them!"

"Wish I could weed a pretty garden like that and maybe pick a few flowers and put them in a tumbler on a table."

"What a silly thing to wish when you can live on a schooner and sail away to places everywhere and see porpoises and whales and vessels from all over the world and storms and everything!"

[6]

"I *hate* drifting round all the time on this old hulk! I want to go some place and stay put and look out of my window every morning and see the same thing."

"Why don't you, then?"

"Why don't you go to sea?"

"Em'ly!" shouted Mrs. Trask in a voice capable of being heard in a gale, let alone above the clatter of the shoppers. "Em'ly, you go catch them shag kittens. Mrs. Decker here thinks she might like one."

The girl left the protection of the wheel and disappeared towards the bow, bringing back with her a box from which four or five heads of dandelion yellow, with short kitten ears, were popping up, while soft paws clawed at the edges and had to be pushed back.

Mrs. Decker wasted no time. "I'll take that double-pawed one with the white nose. But I won't pay more'n a quarter for any cat or kitten under heaven."

Mrs. Trask didn't argue the point.

"You'll have to put it in your shopping basket," she said. "My paper bags are giving out. I got that lot of kittens over at Boothbay. Party I got them from said the old cat was a fine ratter."

Elderly Mr. Young stood watching the kittens for a while, and then took out a quarter and gave

[7]

it to Emily, and picked up the smallest kitten and put in into his pocket.

"Why, Mr. Young, what do you want another cat for?" Ken asked. "You got five now. Five anyhow and maybe more."

Elderly Mr. Young winked at the children.

"Just had a fancy for a foreign cat. Know all the ways of the ones 'round Friendship. Come on, Barley, you and me'd better go home," and he made his way through the women and up the gangplank.

"He's real nice," Ken explained. "He lets us take as many apples from his trees as we've a mind to."

Emily was twirling a straw for the remaining kittens and said in a softened voice, "I liked him."

But there was no getting away from Belle Trask's demands.

"Here, you, Em'ly! Put them kittens away. I want you should run up the rigging and get that clothes-basket for Mrs. Thomson."

"That's too high for you," Ken began, but Emily interrupted him.

"Wish I had a penny for every time I've climbed clear up to the topsail. You take the kittens back. There's a crate top to put over them."

"Em'ly!" shouted Mrs. Trask.

Without answering, Emily climbed into the rigging, detached the clothesbasket, which looked almost as large as she was, and composedly climbed down again to give it to Mrs. Trask.

"While you're at it, bring down that second shovel, Em'ly," called Cliff Trask from where he was talking with one of the Simmons boys.

"And hurry, Em'ly!" shouted Mrs. Trask. "I want you should go down in the cabin—they're clamoring for attention in there."

Ken didn't see the new girl for some time, as he wasn't interested in cabins, but *was* interested in everything else about a vessel. He looked the old *Pluribus* over from stem to stern, shaking his head over the condition of the eagle at the bowsprit, coiling a line now and then as he came across one that needed coiling. Cliff Trask was a good seaman, but the women came aboard so fast, it didn't give him time to get the deck shipshape when he first tied up at a wharf. He'd have her all redded up before he left in a few days, but meanwhile Ken lent a hand. It was funny. Nothing on board ship seemed like work. But everything ashore did, even working round the shop with Dad and the boys. Ken would get so mad, thinking how he'd never sail on the sloop they were building, that he'd sneak away from the boat shop every chance he could get and go fishing in the pea-pod.

Someone had to fish.

[9]

When Dad scolded, Ma'd say, "At least Ken don't waste his time. There's two or three nice pollock in the ice house, not counting what's in the skillet for your dinner," and that would kind of take the edge off Dad's annoyance.

Ralph and Stuart used to try to reason with him, telling him there was twice the money in boat building there was in going to sea, but they gave it up. It was like talking to a cod. Ken just looked at nothing and set his jaw and they knew he wasn't listening. Made Ralph kind of mad, but Stuart was easy-going.

"I tell you what, Ken, Ralph and me'll build you a sloop of your own when you're twenty-one," he promised, but eight years is a terribly long time to wait when a boy is crazy to go to sea.

Chapter Two

MRS. PHILBROOK was full of talk of the store boat that noon, who had been there and what everyone had bought.

"And there was a little girl, Otis, they'd got from the Portland orphan asylum. Did you notice, Ken, she had one blue eye and one hazel eye? She was pretty, just the same, but not happy looking. If I didn't know Cliff and Belle Trask so well, I'd say they weren't treating her right."

Ken looked up from his plate of corned beef, onions, carrots, potatoes, and cabbage.

"She's silly," he said. "Doesn't like going to sea, that's all."

"There's lots of people feel the same way," Mrs. Philbrook ruminated. "I've got a cousin on Gott's Island never's been off the island. Husband can't persuade her to try it."

"Just give me the chance," said Ken to his plate. He had given up saying it to his family.

"Well, Nabby, what did you buy with your three dollars?" Mr. Philbrook asked, when the pie and cake had been cleared off the table.

Mrs. Philbrook had been waiting for the question.

"It's all over there on the sideboard. Half a dozen spools of thread, new knitting needles, a dipper, and a fresh wash bowl for the back-porch bench—the old one looks bad, it's so chipped—and a saucepan in place of the one that got left on the stove last winter."

"Looks like you'd got your money's worth. Wasn't there anything you wanted for yourself?"

Mrs. Philbrook smiled and patted down her apron.

"Yes, Otis," she said gently, "there was quite a little more it seemed to me we needed. I got a nice pattern of white organdy for a summer church-going dress and a chip hat to match and some cotton to make you and the boys shirts out of and buttons and half a dozen sheets and pillow cases and I guess that's about all!"

"Whew! Ma! That's a whole lot at once. Guess you'll have to go into your egg money."

Stuart winked at Ralph, who winked back. They had heard this conversation every year for as far back as they could remember and knew just how it would end, but Ken, who hadn't lived so long, listened rather anxiously. He had forty-seven cents of his own if that would help Ma out.

But Mrs. Philbrook was as smiling as ever.

"Why, Otis, you know the egg money's for specials. These things have to be got. I guess nobody's going to say that Otis Philbrook's wife puts patched sheets on her line, and you certainly don't want to be ashamed of me when we go to church."

"Your pink dress looks nice as far as I can see."

"Men don't see far. Everyone's seen that old pink dress till they're sick and tired of it."

Mr. Philbrook might have said more, but Stuart pushed back his chair, followed by Ralph.

"Guess we'll be getting along, Dad. Want to finish putting in that decking today if we can."

Mr. Philbrook surrendered. "How much will it come to, Nabby?"

"Seventeen dollars and forty-five cents. The little girl's going to bring the things up this afternoon. Seventeen dollars will do. I'll take the rest out of the egg money."

No one was surprised when Mr. Philbrook carefully counted out twenty dollars.

"Might as well be hung for a sheep as a lamb,"

he said, giving Mrs. Philbrook a little pat on the shoulder. "Like as not Belle's got something more you've set your heart on."

For once Ken tagged his father down the path worn between the house and the boat shop on the shore. The gulls were flying back and forth overhead, silently, as white as angels and as graceful. The green-black spruces darkened the land, below which the bay, circled close by islands, sparkled with every ruffling of the water.

"Dad," Ken said, but his father didn't hear. He was watching the gulls as he often did, as he would watch a fish or a porpoise for that matter, studying the creature's beautiful strong shape, wondering how he could learn from it, so that the next sloop he built would be lighter and swifter in the water than the last. Other people were well satisfied with the vessels he built, but Mr. Philbrook tugged at his pale mustache and was never satisfied. For the sloop must be safe, as well as fast. For he did not forget that men were to sail her, and that on his head lay the responsibility for his neighbors' lives.

"Dad," Ken repeated, pulling at his father's old coat.

Mr. Philbrook looked down. "What can I do for you, son?"

"Lend me some white paint, Dad?"

"Do you mean lend or give?"

Ken grinned. "Give me some white paint, Dad?"

"How much?"

"Nuff to paint the eagle on the *Pluribus.*"

"Do you think Cliff'll trust you? Guess he will. It needs paint all right. Last time I saw it, the old bird looked like he was moulting. You can have half a can."

By this time they had reached the shadows of the half open shed, where Ralph and Stuart were outlined dark on the bright water beyond.

"Hey!" yelled Ralph sharply. "That's my best brush, Ken. Take one of those in the corner."

"When I get the white on, I'll need blue for the ribbon and red for the stripes on the shield."

"I heard you."

"And a *little* yellow for his beak and claws, Dad."

"And a *little* green for the leaves. Guess we can spare that much for the American eagle. But you won't need much, Ken! There's no use wasting good paint. Hunt up some old cans, and we'll pour a little in, and you'd better take a couple more of the small brushes. But wash them out when you're through and *bring them back.*"

Ken hurried off between the first goldenrod and the last daisies.

"Wish he'd show as much interest in the sloops,"

Stuart said from the upper shadows, where he was sitting on his heels, laying deck slowly and carefully.

"He would, if they were afloat," Mr. Philbrook answered, taking up his tools. "Sometimes I think we'll have to let him go, but I don't like to worry Ma."

"Nothing worries Ma," said Ralph, halfway up the ladder.

"I'm afraid this would."

No more was said on the subject, as the three were soon lost in their work. Ken heard the tap, tap of hammers and the squeal of a saw as he reached the road, but the sounds were as familiar to him as the mewing scream of the gulls, and he never thought about them.

He carried the clumsy clam basket carefully, with its load of old tins into which the paints had been poured. He was absorbed in a vision of the eagle of the *E Pluribus Unum,* bright and gay and proud once more, and nearly ran into the girl Emily, who was coming up the road with her arms filled with heavy packages. Ma was right. She *did* have one blue eye and one brown one.

"Hello, Ken," she said, cheerfully for her. "I was hoping I'd meet you. Up here all the houses look alike. Which is yours? I've got a lot of things for your ma."

Ken turned round and pointed out his house.

"Up there, under the eaves, it has one of those big wooden cobwebby things. Ours has a star on it. Bents' has a kind of sunflower, and Smalls' has fans. You can tell by that if you don't remember the shapes. Of course, they're all white."

Emily stared at the houses. "I never noticed how fancy they are," she said admiringly. "That doily thing up there dresses them up a lot. And some have the wooden lacework all along the edges of the roofs, but I like yours best. A star is nice."

"I'm going down to the store boat and see if I can't paint up that old eagle. Wouldn't you like that?"

"I don't know's I care. I suppose it *would* look better."

"I hope the Trasks will let me."

"They'll let you. Your ma bought a lot of things. I'd better be getting on or I'll drop them."

" 'By, Emily."

" 'By, Ken."

Clifford Trask was perfectly willing to let Ken have a try at the eagle. He watched him a little while, to make sure he was careful with his paint, and then wandered back to his customers. People

[18]

were still coming aboard the *E Pluribus Unum* but by now there was more gossiping and less buying.

No one came near Ken. All the long afternoon he worked, whistling to himself in short sharp breaths, shrill and tuneless, utterly absorbed in the slow transformation taking place under his hands. At first he was not quite sure of himself and several times had to swab off a blob of paint which had appeared in the wrong place, but as he gained in confidence there were no more accidents. The lean head, the spread wings, and strong legs of the bird stood out now from the faded bow of the schooner, and with mounting excitement Ken saw the fresh green laurel leaves, the shield, and the lettering appear.

It was very late in the afternoon before he had finished, and Belle Trask walked up to admire his handiwork.

"That does brighten her up a whole lot," she said. "Cliff and I are obliged to you. It's good for trade, and then—well, it just looks nice. We get too busy to notice. Maybe this fall when we lay up at Swan's Island we can have her all painted. Thanks a lot."

"That's all right," said Ken bashfully. "I liked doing it."

"You're the Philbrook boy, aren't you? I remember you other years. Wish that Em'ly would take an interest like you do." She sighed. "That reminds me, she isn't back yet. You tell her if you see her to come right along. She's not supposed to take half a day when she goes on an errand."

Now that the customers had all gone home the remaining kittens had the run of the deck and were scampering about wildly, chasing one another, bouncing up in the air, their soft fur ruffled to make them look twice their size, rushing out of hiding places to clutch one another in pretended fury, which sometimes became so nearly real that two kittens would roll together into the scuppers and then dash apart, their little tails straight up in the air.

A pleasant smell of baked beans came from the cabin, and the small ripples slapped gently against the schooner's sides. All the shadows were very long. The whole village lay in shadow, with the roofs and trees like ornaments against a golden sky, but the islands were bright with late sunshine, and the seagulls, floating in the upper air, were rosy pink, not white at all.

Ken felt an almost unbearable heaviness of heart as he walked slowly away from the store boat. He kicked sadly at the stones in the path. Earth meant nothing to him, so strong and deep in him was the love of the sea. He turned back to look at the eagle he had painted, and the great bird seemed almost ready to fly away, away to some other harbor, some small inlet in an island, or tucked away along the shore of a point, places which Ken had never seen and perhaps would never see.

When he got home he found Emily still in the kitchen with his mother, who looked up with an air of preoccupied pleasure.

"Been teaching Emily how to make my gingerbread," she explained. "She's real quick at catching on."

Emily looked like another girl, so happy and eager.

"May I give Ken a piece, ma'am?" she asked. "It's the first I ever made."

Ken had a moment's qualm about delivering Belle Trask's message. He knew that as soon as he mentioned the store boat she'd change back into the old Emily; but if he didn't, she might get into trouble.

He took a bite of gingerbread.

"That's good," he said. "Real good, Emily. You'd better take some back for the Trasks, if Ma doesn't mind. Belle said to tell you you were wanted."

The light faded out of Emily's two-colored eyes, the smile drained from her lips.

"Oh, dear!" she exclaimed anxiously. "They'll be put out! Here I've gone and forgotten again. I can't keep track of time once I get ashore. Thank you, Mrs. Philbrook, for everything. I've never had such a happy afternoon," and she hurried towards the door.

"Wait a minute!" called Mrs. Philbrook. "Ken, you find a paper bag folded up on the second pantry shelf. I want you to take the gingerbread, Emily. And come back if you can. I don't know when *I've* had such a pleasant afternoon either." And cutting the gingerbread free from the pan with an expert hand, she put it neatly into the paper bag which Ken had brought, and, as she handed it to Emily, leaned down and kissed her.

The girl flung her arms about her and began to cry. Then she pulled herself free and said, almost desperately, "I'd better get going now, if I'm going to go," and ran out, slamming the screen door behind her.

"She isn't very polite," said Ken, "and that gingerbread will be all crumbs."

His mother didn't answer. She was standing, the knife still in her hand, looking out of the window after Emily. Then she shook her head, sighed, and turned back to the business of getting supper.

Chapter Three

W E'RE sailing tomorrow," said Cliff Trask at early breakfast. "I kind of think, Belle, we ought to hire a rig and drive up to Waldoboro and get some new merchandise. They've cleaned us pretty well out of dress goods and men's shoes, and we're low on nails and screws, too."

"If we're going, we might's well go to Thomaston. It's not much further and we can buy cheaper," said his wife. "We'd better get an early start. Em'ly can tend the boat. There won't be many people now we've been here five days. But you mind what I say, Em'ly! You stay right aboard all the time we're gone and don't you go wool-gathering off ashore. The people of Friendship are as honest as they come, but there's bound to be one or two bad apples in any barrel, and there's a valuable cargo aboard as you well know."

"Yes'm," said Emily, looking at nothing and no one.

Belle Trask reached over and shook her, not unkindly. "Wake up, Em'ly! Wake up! Now mind what I say. Don't you leave the schooner, you hear me?"

"Yes'm," repeated Emily in the same dead-alive voice.

"Honestly, you'd try the patience of a saint!" cried Belle.

"She heard you," Cliff interposed. "She won't leave, will you, Em'ly? But you and me'd better be starting, Belle. I spoke yesterday to Luke Genthner, and he said we could have his rig."

Belle put on her bonnet and shawl but she was still uneasy as she went down the gangplank after her husband.

"Em'ly, you sweep up the deck and clean up the cabin. And polish the lucky dollar. I noticed it's getting dull-looking. And there's some clams in the pail for your dinner and all the bread you need. Now you remember my words. You stay aboard this schooner and don't set foot even on the wharf," she added, looking back as she slowly walked away.

"Yes'm," said Emily, scarcely lifting her eyes.

At last Mrs. Trask was driven to threats.

"You do what I say or you'll get what-for!" she called back darkly.

"Yes'm," agreed Emily.

"That girl!" said Mrs. Trask to her husband as she joined him. "She's like heavy dough. I thought after we'd had her for a while she'd lighten up, but she's heavy as she ever was. I think we'd better take her back to the asylum this fall and see if we can't get one who'll suit us better."

"Just as you say. Maybe we might try a boy this time."

"Anything'd be better than Em'ly. She's all right in herself, but not with us, somehow."

"Yes, she's a good shoe, but she don't fit our foot," agreed Cliff Trask. "We'd be better off with someone else, and she'd be better off, too. It's kind of a pity when anyone as young as Em'ly ain't happy."

"She don't *try* to be happy!" snapped Mrs. Trask, but later, as she settled into the seat beside her husband and the team started off, she said in a gentler voice, "I don't know as Em'ly *can* be happy at sea. She's got such a hankering for the land."

Emily, left alone in the early morning, began her work valiantly. She swept the deck first, so that she could keep an eye on the village and watch it waking up as the smoke appeared like a plume, first from one chimney, and then another, and small distant doors opened upon small figures of men emerging, with milking pails which winked in the newborn light. Cocks crowed, answering one another, and a dog barked excitedly as a boy ran down the slope to the shore, bent probably on fishing. Now came an occasional pounding as stakes were driven into the damp earth for hitching out cows, and a calf bawled after its mother, and a woman called her family in to breakfast.

The little village, high above the harbor, seemed to shine in white paint, outlined on green fields. The sheds were red, with gilded weathervanes, and there were flowers in the shelter of the ells. To Emily, mechanically sweeping the deck of the *E Pluribus*

Unum, Friendship looked like a village in heaven, with the July light of heaven shining upon it.

Her eye swept with disdain past the wharf to the fish houses beyond, with their bait tubs and lobster pots and the painted markers hung against their old shingles. She hated the smell of bait and tar and dead fish which rose all around her. But along the shore there were little paths and raspberry thickets, where the fruit was ripe now, for she had seen some women in sunbonnets picking there only yesterday.

A man rowed past her, standing at the oars and facing the way he was going. He nodded to her and she nodded back to him, but he was a fisherman and the people who interested her were the happy people moving about the houses. At last, with a sigh, she began sweeping the rest of the deck, but even here she could watch the islands, which were so near that she could hear a robin singing in an oak tree by the shore.

When the day had advanced a little, she fed the kittens and played with them for a while. Then she brought a cloth and polished the dollar fastened to the mast. Clifford Trask, who had nailed it there twenty years ago, set great store by it.

"If that dollar ever left the schooner, all our luck would go with it," he used to say. Emily knew that it was the first money he had taken in over the counter when he opened his shop. The schooner was named for it, and was built in the year the dollar was minted. So long as that dollar was safely nailed to the mast, there'd be no lack of dollars in Cliff Trask's pocket and Belle Trask's pocketbook.

So Emily polished carefully, if with little enthusiasm, and then, sighing sadly, went with heavy feet down into the cabin to make the narrow bunks and wash the thick dishes.

No one came aboard all the morning, except for a little girl sent to buy a spool of white thread, and she ran right off with it because she said that her mother was waiting all ready to thread her needle as soon as she got home.

Emily had her dinner alone, except for the kittens. Her work was done, the Trasks wouldn't be back until early evening.

"Sometime before sunset, or soon after," Belle Trask had said.

Now there was nothing for Emily to do. It was hot. The *Pluribus* was slowly settling as the tide went out and the wet mud flats began to appear along the shores. Most of the fishing boats had left long ago, and the wharves were deserted, except for an old man or two sitting on shaded benches by distant fish houses, whittling.

With all her heart and soul Emily longed for the

[28]

land. She wanted to go back to Mrs. Philbrook's kitchen, to see Ken again, to hear the pleasant sounds of building from the boat yard below, as she talked with Mrs. Philbrook. But Belle Trask had told her not to set foot so much as on the wharf. But if she went to the shore where the wild raspberries were growing, she could keep her eye on the *Pluribus* while she worked. She would face towards the harbor. A mouse couldn't get aboard without her seeing it. What could be the harm of that?

Emily found an empty lard pail and went ashore. The tide was so low she had to climb up on the rail, and from there scramble to the wharf, but she was nimble. With heart beating guiltily, she hurried to the shore and turned right, to where the raspberries grew at the foot of the meadow.

Though there had been pickers the day before, none came this hot afternoon, and Emily had the place to herself. At first she looked up at the schooner between every berry or two, but the quiet afternoon lulled her, and she didn't see the man and big boy in sea boots until they were standing right over the *Pluribus,* looking down at her deck, and the man had called, not very loud, "Ahoy there! anyone aboard?"

Emily piped up in her clear voice from the shore, "Want anything, mister?"

At the sound of her voice, the man swung around and studied her for a minute in silence.

Then he said, "Nope, I guess not. Just wanted to see if your folks would like some clams."

She saw then that the big boy was carrying a pail.

"We got all the clams we can use," she called back and then added, "I'm sorry."

The man didn't answer, but the two walked off and disappeared. Emily, watching them, noticed that the pail was leaky.

"They'd better put some more water in that pail or the clams'll die," she thought. "Wonder he didn't buy a new one. Too poor, maybe."

For the two had seemed poor, or at least as though they didn't have a woman to look after them. Somehow, they didn't walk or talk quite like the other people in Friendship. But she was more interested in her raspberries than in strangers, and forgot them as soon as they were out of sight.

There were perhaps not very many ripe berries, but the ones she found were large and delicious. There were birds in the thickets, too, which flew up with a whir of wings, and the swallows were skimming back and forth across the summer clouds, now high, now low, and the young bobolinks were perched on the goldenrod stems, while one old bird sang from the dark summit of a spruce.

After a while she came to a small thicket, and in it she found something delightful. It was a pilot house, taken from some old vessel named the *Thomas E. Bailey* and brought ashore and put under a pine tree, from whose roots rose a very small spring of clear water where the bunchberries grew thick. The whole front of the little building was of glass, and inside Emily could see a small stove set against the back wall and an army cot with a couple of old patchwork quilts on it. There was a pile of paper-backed books on a shelf with some china, a bow with its arrows in a corner, a big colored picture of a four-master tacked on the wall, not quite straight, and a rusty skillet on the stove.

Emily gave a delighted look and hurried back to the field to make sure that the schooner was all right. She could see all the deck except for a little space behind the cabin. The remaining tin pans and pails shone in the shrouds, the brooms and mops hung in their depleted clusters. All was well. She ducked back to explore the building she had discovered.

At her touch the handle turned and the door swung open, letting her in to a hot and airless little room. Dust lay on everything; in the corners spiders sat in their webs, watching her. No one had slept in that bed for a long time.

She picked up a book with a picture on the cover of boats leaving a burning ship. "Ken P." was written on the first page, and then in a straggling handwriting came:

"Steal not this book my honest friend
For fear the gallows will be thy end."

"I suppose his pa put this up here for Ken sometime, and maybe he used it a lot for a while and then got tired of it. Wish I had time to give it a good redding up," she thought.

But she didn't have time. Always the Trasks were at the back of her mind and Belle's repeated warnings. Maybe she hadn't done quite what Belle wanted, but she'd certainly kept an eye on the store boat, anyway.

As she went out, closing the door carefully behind her, she noticed that the path through the grove was nearly overgrown. That Ken! Always hankering after water. Didn't seem to realize that the only good craft is a craft ashore.

Emily picked berries for a while longer and then sat in the field with a view of the schooner and watched swallows and ants and ladybugs and a woman hanging out clothes on a line at a house close by the shore of the nearest island.

When the sun began to get low, Emily knew she'd better return, or the Trasks might catch her on shore and there'd be a terrible scene. Belle wasn't an unkind woman, but she had a rough tongue when her temper was roused, and she'd have a right to be mad if anyone deliberately went and disobeyed her the way Emily had.

"She's never licked me yet," Emily thought, "but if she found me off the *Pluribus*, she would this time and I wouldn't blame her. I'd better eat the rest of the berries and get aboard quick and get my face and hands washed. Hope I haven't got any stains on my dress."

A little uneasily she trotted down the wharf and lowered herself onto the *Pluribus*. The tide was only beginning to rise and there was still a steep descent. The kittens rushed to meet her, mewing pathetically.

"Where have you been?" their thin little voices asked. "Where have you been?" for they had never been left alone before.

Emily picked them up, comforting them with small loving noises. Here she was back again in her prison. She glanced about her with experienced eyes.

Mercy, what was that? She was sure that there had been a pail hanging there, just within reach. But it was gone! And there were four brooms instead of five, and only one clam rake left and an axe was gone and a hoe and goodness knows what else. But she had never been out of sight for more than three minutes at a time. Could someone have rowed up on the further side and thrown up a rope and climbed aboard, keeping the cabin between him and her figure on the shore?

And two or three overalls were gone from the cabin and a blanket. Oh, oh, oh, oh! In blind terror Emily ran back on deck. As she passed the mast, her tear-filled eyes were aware that something further was wrong, something far more serious even than the disappearance of so much merchandise. The 1872 dollar had been wrenched from its nail, and now only a circle of varnished, lighter wood showed where it had once been. U. S. 739049

The luck of the *E Pluribus Unum* was gone.

And just then Emily heard the well-known voices of Cliff and Belle Trask above the rattle of a surrey, as it came down the steep hill from the village.

Chapter Four

KEN had, on the whole, had a pretty unsatisfactory day. When he saw the Trasks drive by in Luke Genthner's rig early that morning, he'd had it in mind to go down to see Emily and the store boat and have a look at the eagle to see if it looked as it had when he painted it. But his father and mother seemed bound and determined to spoil his day.

It was "Ken, run get me a half-pound box of Lipton's tea and a bag of salt at Mrs. Drew's, and I mean now!" from Ma and it was "Ken, we need some clearing up round the shop. 'Spose you could sweep up the shavings and stack the odds and ends for kindling this morning?" from Dad and it was "Fetch this" and "Hand me that" from Ralph and Stuart, and then a whole family of cousins had driven over to see them from Nobleboro, and while the men were looking over the sloop and Dad was explaining all the changes he was making and Cousin

[36]

Edith was talking to Ma, rocking on the porch, he had to entertain a whining boy cousin and two girls who lugged dolls around with them everywhere they went and were afraid even to get into a dory.

"They'll have to go home early," Ken thought hopefully. "Cousin Ed's got the cows to milk," but Cousin Ed had made an arrangement about the milking with his next-door neighbor, and they didn't actually go until nearly five o'clock, after two or three false starts.

Ken waved them off, as in duty bound, and then bolted before anyone could ask him to do anything else. He had some bait and a fishline in the pea-pod, keeping cool under the seat, and he had been thinking of fishing all day. It was still quite low tide, but by that time most of the flats were covered, though he could see the bottom clearly through the shallow water. His flat-bottomed, square-ended little boat could go almost anywhere. He moseyed along. Once he stopped for some time to watch a foot-long squid, on a bed of seaweed out of the water. He couldn't imagine how it had got there, but it kept quivering and turning from scarlet to emerald green, to violet, to blue. He had never seen anything like it before, with its short tentacles and flat, almost anchor-shaped tail, so ugly in shape and so strangely beautiful in color. When at last the creature turned white, he realized that it was dead and rowed on along the shore.

He could see through the water where Alonzo Durgin had pulled out his dory. There was the narrow groove where the keel had scraped and the oozy print of his boots. Then, beyond, he could see where Dale Fraser and Young Dale had been clamming. There were the footprints and the bottom dug-up in patterns. He hoped, vaguely, they'd got a good haul. They always looked so ragged, ever since they'd arrived last summer from up coast and camped out in old Mr. Young's fish house which he wasn't using any more. Dad said he knew they were the ones who'd taken a lot of his potatoes and beets out of the garden last year, but he guessed he could spare something if folks needed it that bad, and this year he'd planted some extra, counting they'd take it. Ma said they were shiftless and she wouldn't be surprised any day if they sneaked something off her line, but she mended up an old coat of Dad's and some trousers and a sweater of Ralph's and sent them down to the Frasers by Ken. They looked real neat when Ma'd got through with them, but they were all in rags like the rest of their stuff before the Frasers had worn them a month.

Ken could see the round marks where the pails had stood while they were being filled. There was a lot a person could tell just by tracks. And then he saw something that looked small and white, like a sand dollar, and yet different. It was right beside some of the dug-up bottom.

"What in creation?" thought Ken and, giving one oar a tug, he reached overboard and down into the cold clear water and at his first attempt brought up the 1872 dollar. He recognized it at first glance.

"How did it ever get there?" he thought. The coin was twisted a little, as if it had been wrenched from its heavy nail, but he would know it anywhere, with the hole in the middle. What was it doing off the schooner? And what did the Frasers have to do with it?

[39]

The day was beginning to darken with late afternoon clouds, black in the west. It had been hot, and now there was the promise of a thunderstorm in the air. Ken looked over his shoulder towards the store boat and was surprised to see a girl's figure running along the wharf towards the shore.

It must be Emily, he thought. There was trouble of some kind aboard and he'd better go over, but, rowing, he lost sight of the short gingham dress he had seen, bright in the last light before the storm. He was some distance up harbor, and, by the time he hailed the *Pluribus,* there was no sign whatever of Emily, but Genthner's rig was on the wharf and Clifford and Belle Trask were running around the deck, sometimes yelling to each other about some new thing that had been taken and sometimes hollering for Emily.

When Ken appeared with the lucky dollar, they both felt better. The first thing Cliff did was to straighten it out on an anvil he had, covering it first with felt, and then he nailed it back in its place on the mast.

"Now things will work out," he said. "First tell us just where you found it, Ken."

So Ken told him, his blue eyes snapping with excitement.

"Looks like Em'ly had been ashore after all—"

"I *knew* she'd leave the boat," said Belle. "I'm sick and tired of that girl."

"And someone sneaked onto the *Pluribus*, maybe up the side, and stole what he wanted—mostly things a clammer would like when I come to think of it. How do you figure the dollar got in the water?"

"His clothes are always full of holes, and probably it worked through a hole in his pocket while he was busy digging, and he never noticed."

"Looks like a case for the sheriff. Who's sheriff here?"

"Carl Vinal."

"We'll go have a talk with him. Want to come, Belle? We'll get someone to keep the boat while we're away."

The Trasks quickly unloaded their purchases and locked them into the cabin. By now half a dozen men and boys, scenting trouble as seagulls scent fish, had gathered, and Cliff chose an acquaintance to stay aboard. He didn't tell anyone what had happened, but by the time he had picked up Carl Vinal in the Genthner rig and driven down to the Fraser fish house, word had somehow reached the clammers that the law was closing in upon them, for they had gone off in a hurry, leaving their supper half eaten on the table and the stove going full blast. They had also left behind most of the stolen loot, which Cliff and Belle identified.

By this time the thunder was rolling and roaring continually back of the village, and a deep dusk had closed in so that one could not even see the islands. The first lamps had been lighted in the houses, and, though a few streaks of pale yellow showed below the clouds, it would be dark in half an hour, except where the lightning was beginning to fork down the airy terraces of the clouds.

"We got almost everything back, except a couple of hunting knives and a dollar watch," said Belle, looking around. "It don't look like these folks had much themselves, does it, Cliff?"

"No," said Cliff. "I'm satisfied, Mr. Vinal. Why don't we let the matter drop? We don't want to prosecute. It would never have happened in the first place if that girl of ours had stayed where she belonged."

Ken, who had, of course, gone along with the Trasks, now spoke up.

"Where *is* Emily?"

"Yes, where *is* she?" repeated Belle. "She'd slipped my mind in the excitement, but we've got to find her. It's beginning to rain, too, and getting black as the inside of a cow."

Chapter Five

~~~~~~

IT WAS easy to talk about finding Emily, but Emily was not easy to find. The Genthner horses were afraid of the storm. If they hadn't been tired from the all-day trip, they'd probably have bolted. As it was, they reared several times, and backed when the lightning came especially close, and nearly upset the surrey. Everyone was glad to get them safely back to their stable and take up the search on foot.

"I'll bet she's on the *Pluribus* this minute," Belle suggested. "No girl's going to hide under a bush long in a storm like this."

But when they went back to the schooner, there was no sign of Emily, though they called and searched.

"Maybe she's gone up to your house, Ken," Cliff suggested. "We'd better go up and see. Belle, you stay here and get some dry clothes on. We'll be back in just a few minutes."

"No, I'll go along. I've been wet before."

"Put on your slicker and sou-wester then."

"I'm wet as an eel already. Let's start. No good standing here talking."

As they climbed up the road she asked Ken, "Em'ly and your ma get on well?"

"Sure," said Ken. He hadn't thought much about it, but now he remembered his mother kissing Emily and the way the girl had clung to her, almost like a kitten he once saved from drowning. He'd pushed an oar out to it, and it had hung on desperately —a little the way Emily looked, now he thought of it.

"Real well," he said.

"I just hope she's with your ma then," said Belle, sloshing ahead. The sheriff had left them, telling them to be sure to let him know if they didn't find the girl.

"She may have started back to Waldoboro," Cliff suggested uneasily. "There's miles without a house, and she may be lost. Or she might have started out for Thomaston, even."

"Swamps," said Belle. "I wish I hadn't tried to scare her about leaving the schooner. She ought to know my bark's a lot worse than my bite."

"Now don't you start blaming yourself, Belle," her husband comforted her. "You didn't say anything to frighten anyone. She frightened herself when she saw the stuff had been stolen."

"Here we are," said Ken, turning in at the gate. Through the rain the kitchen windows looked so peaceful, all yellow with lamplight. But when the three of them appeared, soaking, at the door, they found only Mr. Philbrook reading the Portland paper and Mrs. Philbrook darning socks on the other side of the table, while the two big boys played cribbage.

"No, she hasn't been here," Mrs. Philbrook said anxiously. "Do come in, Mrs. Trask. Why, you're wet to the skin. I'll make you a nice hot cup of tea right away."

Mr. Philbrook glanced at his elder sons and all three, without a word, got up and took their caps and slickers from the woodshed, and lighted a couple of lanterns.

"We'll look around," Mr. Philbrook said. "Ken, you'd better stay in now and change. We'll go with Cliff."

"Please, Dad," Ken began to protest, but his father cut him short, "Do as you're told, son," and the four men went out. For a while the three in the kitchen could hear their voices calling through the slash of rain and the thunder, but soon there was only the storm sluicing at the windows.

"Why do things always have to happen in storms?" Mrs. Philbrook asked. "Ken, you go change like a good boy. Your tea's almost ready, Mrs. Trask."

Ken did change and stood at the window, his freckled nose flattened against the pane. Like the women, he was uneasy and restless. He saw Emily's face and her unhappy two-colored eyes. A storm like this wasn't anything for a girl to be out in. She was going towards the shore when he'd seen her. Running. She'd already been ashore, the Trasks said. Where'd she been? If he'd been in her place what would he have been doing? But of course, *he*'d have been in a boat. But if he'd been on land?

Guiltily he went into the shed and put on his own slicker and let himself out. His dad and the others must have been away an hour. Once he thought he heard someone calling "Em'ly!" over by the point. The rain was not coming so hard now and he could count nine or ten between lightning and thunder so the storm was passing by. The grass was slippery underfoot and cool against his legs. He followed the path towards the shop and then branched off on a much less worn path that struck down harbor. Sometimes there didn't seem any path at all. Two years ago there'd been a good one, but he didn't go down to the *Thomas E. Bailey* very often these days. Still, he'd have known the way even without the lightning.

In the clump of trees and bushes the ground was almost dry again, though rain kept spattering down on his shoulders. The pilot house was dark, but when he opened the door and called "Emily," something stirred inside and her voice faltered, "Who's that?"

"You come right out of there this minute," he said severely. "You've had everyone hunting for you for hours and scared half to death."

"About *me*?" Emily quavered. "I didn't think anybody'd care two straws. If I hadn't been too scared, I'd have run up to your house when it began splitting and spitting so."

"Well, you're going to my house now. Put one of those quilts over you. It's still raining. And hurry up. Belle Trask is waiting."

Emily drew back again. "Oh, Ken, I don't dare."

"What are you scared of Belle for? She's not going to eat you. She's real nice. Oh, yes. You don't know. They got all the things, or almost all, back again. You're what they've been worrying about."

He could hear her splashing and stumbling up the overgrown path behind him.

"And the lucky dollar?" came her anxious voice.

Ken expanded. "I found that. Right under a foot and a half of water where Dale Fraser'd been digging clams. That's how come they got all the rest of the things."

"How wonderful!"

When they had reached the wider path she asked, "Was your ma worried, too?"

"Sure she was worried," he answered impatiently. Then he remembered her drowning kitten look and added gently, "Real worried, Emily."

When the children came into the kitchen door, there was great excitement. Belle burst into tears of relief and the next moment would have boxed Emily's ears if Mrs. Philbrook hadn't interfered.

"The child's been through as much as you have," she said. "She's skin and bones. Sea life don't agree with Emily. She ought to stay ashore."

"I'll go and blow the horn for Dad," Ken interposed. "Come on, Emily, it's in the shed."

The repeated blare of the dinner horn brought the men in after a time.

"Well, young lady, you've had us all by the ears," exclaimed Cliff Trask good-humoredly when he saw Emily. "Once is all right, but don't you do it again. It could get tiresome. Who found you? Ken? Ken, you're quite a boy. Found the lucky dollar, and that found the loot, and now you've found Emily. Wish I could do something for you in return."

The desires of a lifetime rose up in Kenneth Philbrook like a racing tide.

"Wish you could take me on the *Pluribus*, Cliff. I'd work hard."

Cliff Trask laughed.

"Wish we could, Ken. Belle and me'd like nothing better, but I guess your pa and ma'd have a word to say about that."

When Ken spoke, his mother had taken a quick deep breath and stopped darning, her needle in the air.

Now she looked at her husband, who looked at her.

"It's up to his ma," said Mr. Philbrook.

Mrs. Philbrook didn't speak right away. Then she smiled.

"I've seen it coming a long time," she said in her ordinary voice. "Most of the men in Otis' family, and mine, too, have been sailors. If Ken has to go to sea, I'd rather he'd go in the store boat. And when you winter up at Swan's Island, he can come home and have his schooling with us till spring."

"That's fine!" exclaimed Cliff. "Ken's just what we've been looking for, ain't he, Belle?"

"Yes," said Belle. "He likes the sea. Guess we'd

best go down to Portland and take Emily back. Getting her was my idea, and it hasn't worked out too good."

"To the orphan asylum?" asked Emily in a stricken voice.

"I'm real sorry, but you've only yourself to thank, haven't you? You've been down-spirited right along, and then look at the trouble you've made everyone today."

"Yes," said Emily miserably. "I guess I'm no good."

But Mr. Philbrook's blue eyes and Mrs. Philbrook's brown had again been seeking counsel together, and at her unspoken question he had nodded. Now she said briskly, "How would you like to stay with us, Emily?"

The girl's face flushed red with sudden joy.

"With you? Here?" she cried. "Could I? Until Ken comes back?"

It was Mr. Philbrook who answered.

"No, for always, if both parties are satisfied, and I have no doubts we will be. Ma always wanted a girl along with all our boys and I guess you're the answer. Now don't cry like that, Emily. It's nothing to cry about," and he went over to pat her heaving shoulder.

Mother Philbrook put out her arms and Emily

came into them like a lost thing which has come home.

Belle Trask sniffed audibly.

"Now it's all come out nice," she said. "I'll write the 'sylum and tell them where she is. They have to know. Cliff, we'd best be getting to bed. It must be near midnight, and we'll be off early."

Cliff Trask went to the door and looked out, letting in the cool damp odor of wet earth and grass.

"Rain's nearly over," he reported, "and the air's cooled off nicely. Good-night, everybody. Ken, you'd better be down with your things by five or a little after. Em'ly can get her things then, if she's staying here tonight. Guess you people won't get much sleep. But don't you worry about Ken. So long as the lucky dollar's at the mast, there's nothing will go wrong on the *E Pluribus Unum*."

While the others were shaking hands and saying good-by, Emily and Ken stood side by side, a little shy. Five days ago they'd never laid eyes on each other. And now they were going to be brother and sister. Five days ago they were both unhappy, and now they had everything in the world they'd been longing for. Somehow that old 1872 dollar had fixed it up for them.

Ken was in a generous mood.

"You can use the *Thomas E. Bailey* whenever you

want to," he said in a voice pitched below the conversation of their elders.

"Really, Ken? Oh, I'd love that! I never in all my life had a place of my own."

Her joy moved him to further heights of generosity.

"I don't use it any more. You can have it for keeps."

Before such a gift Emily was speechless. Then she, too, showed what was in her.

"No," she said, "I'll keep it nice for you and have it ready when you come back. I'm going to miss you, Ken."

"Sure," he said, off-hand. "We'll have fun when I get back. I'll tell you all the places I've been to on the *Pluribus* and everything."

"I'd like to hear."

Suddenly the store boat and Cliff and Belle Trask took on a nostalgic sweetness in Emily's eyes. Not for her was their life, but they had brought her to her present happiness. She ran to the door just as Belle was leaving and put out a penitent hand.

"Good-by, ma'am," she said, all in a breath. "Thank you and Mr. Trask for taking me. And I'm sorry I disobeyed you and made you so much trouble."

Belle Trask was not one to rake up old ashes. She shook hands with Emily quite affectionately.

"Yes, Em'ly," she agreed, "you *were* real naughty. But it seems to have worked out fine for everyone concerned. Good-night, now! See you in the morning!"

And from the darkness behind her, Cliff's voice boomed out cheerfully, "See you tomorrow, folks!"

Chapter Six

N<small>EVER</small> saw a finer day," said Ken, sitting cross-legged on the deck in the shadow of the sail. The *E Pluribus Unum* was hardly doing more than drift. She hadn't enough wake to rock a chip of wood, and the mainsail flapped every once in a while and threatened to jib, but Cliff Trask, at the wheel, lazily came awake enough to head the old schooner so that she caught what faint stir of breeze there might be, and the boom stopped seesawing and went back to where it belonged.

Belle Trask, in her breeches and rubber boots and a man's shirt, sat in a kitchen chair beside Ken, paring potatoes into a pail of fresh water. Ken was helping her.

"You say that *every* day," said Belle.

"Can't help it," said Ken. "Maybe it's the weather, or maybe it's being on a vessel, but everything seems too fine to last. Like when you first see a rainbow."

"I know," said Belle. "Cliff and I feel the same way. But, of course, we're middle-aged. Some of the color's naturally wore off for us. But I remember days twenty years ago when we first started cruising the store boat, sometimes I'd just clap out singing so loud Cliff'd say 'They'll hear you in Nova Scotia,' but I couldn't help it."

"Sounded nice, Belle," said Cliff unexpectedly from the stern. "You always had a sweet voice for a big woman."

"Get along with you, Cliff." But Belle was pleased. "Here, Ken, heave the peels over the rail. We've potatoes enough for an army."

Ken got to his feet in his quick-moving way, dislodging a yellow shag kitten which had been asleep against his leg. The kitten blinked and yawned, its pale pink tongue showing in a hard curve between needle-sharp teeth. The rest of the litter had all been sold by now, but Belle had decided to keep Marigold.

Ken dumped the peels overboard and watched them drift away on the smooth water, dimpled with darker green. As he expected, first one seagull and then four more appeared out of nowhere to investigate, squabbling and squawking as they alighted on the surface, their long wings almost touching high over their heads for one second as they landed.

"Someone ought to catch a few fish for supper," said Ken.

"I don't know but we should be putting the gear out on the shrouds. Ought to make Stonington this afternoon, don't you think, Cliff?" Belle objected.

"Not at the speed we're making," said Cliff. "Ken's got time to catch a mess of fish. Going to fish from deck, boy?"

"I'd rather take the pea-pod."

Cliff took a long look around. The *Pluribus* was slowly, very slowly, heading down the spruce-lined shores of Deer Isle, with here and there a detached island broken off from the coast and gone to sea on its own. You could have floated a hollyhock flower on the surface, which made a grand mirror for clouds. Off to the east there was a fog bank, but it had lain there since dawn, scarcely moving, just a lavender-gray shadow on the blue. A cormorant stood on a red buoy, sunning his big dark wings, and a seal's wet head winked in the sunlight above the surface and then disappeared again.

"Don't see why you shouldn't take the boat," said Cliff. "What breeze there has been is dying down. We ain't made fifty feet in the last half hour."

Belle got up from the chair, easing her back. Shading her eyes with her hand, she, too, looked all about the *Pluribus*.

"You don't think that fog might come in?" she asked uneasily.

"Been there all morning," said her husband.

"Well—" said Belle almost unwillingly and, reaching for the handle of the pail, went below without saying anything further.

Cliff chuckled.

"Never seen Belle this way before. She acts like a hen with one duckling now you're aboard. Never worried about that girl Em'ly none. But it's true Em'ly never took to us or the old *Pluribus* either. Homesick for land all the time."

"Emily fits in fine at our place," said Ken, pulling in the pea-pod, hand over hand.

He climbed over the rail and dropped neatly into the little boat. "So long."

"So long." Cliff seemed almost asleep again. Then he raised up to shout. "Keep us well in sight."

"Sure, Cliff," Ken shouted back. "Sure."

Cliff had another thought.

"Got your bait?"

"Sure," called Ken again. He had the oars in the oarlocks by now and was rowing along easily a little to the lee of the store boat. It didn't matter much where he went. But he was so happy he itched to be doing something, to be going somewhere, to be getting something he could give Cliff and Belle.

The old schooner lay becalmed. To Ken she looked beautiful, though many wouldn't have given her a second glance. Her shrouds now were clear of the accumulation of trade goods which they wore coming into harbor. Not a washtub blinded the eye as it caught the sun. Not a hoe made dull music against a spade. The eagle at the bow cast a reflection of new paint on the lazy surface of the sea below. Cliff at the stern was really asleep, with his chair tilted back and his feet dangling over the wheel, and Belle was below decks. The world was all Ken's.

Towheaded, blue-eyed, wiry, he bent to the oars for the pure joy of it. He rowed once around the *Pluribus* to admire her from every angle, then, some of his surplus energy worn off, he found his lines and bait in the shadow of one of the seats and became absorbed in his fishing.

The minutes slipped by and the minutes slipped by, as much alike as ripples that break on a sandy shore. There was nothing to call Ken's attention from his fishing. He didn't know whether ten minutes or an hour had passed, held as he was in the circle of water, below whose surface anything in the whole ocean might lie hidden.

Now and then, he had a bite and several times he caught a fish, knocked its head on the gunwale, unhooked and rebaited, and became absorbed again.

It was some time before he noticed the change that had come into the air. His body was cool long before his mind was aware of it. The sun was still shining, but the heat had gone out of its light. The color of the water was paler and getting paler all the time.

"Chilly," Ken thought, looking up at last. "Fog must be coming in."

The fog had certainly come in. He could see the store boat, like the white dream of a vessel, with the fog spinning a cocoon about her.

"Better be getting back," Ken thought, and just then he heard the bray of the conch shell.

"That's Belle," he thought. "Bet Cliff's still asleep."

Somehow, while he fished, he had drifted further from the *Pluribus* than he had ever intended, but still he had no fears. Glancing over his shoulder to make sure of his direction, he began to row hard. He was a coast boy and knew that once a fog began to come in, it might come in fast.

The second time he looked towards the schooner he could barely see her. And the third time, she was gone.

Ken checked his uneasiness.

"Conch'll guide me," he thought. He could hear

the shell, loud and anxious, bleating through the fog, and every now and then stopped his rowing to listen for it. At first he was sure that he was making straight towards the sound but then he became less sure. It was hard to tell where it was coming from.

In spite of the fog, a breeze had come up, a cold wet moving of the air. In his last glimpse of the *Pluribus* he had seen that Cliff was lowering sail, but even so, the schooner was no longer becalmed. She was drifting, however slowly, and she was completely hidden from sight.

Ken did not give up hope. His rowing warmed him even in the dripping air. The fog now hid the sun entirely. It was coming so thick that he could scarcely see even the dead dull surface of the water. A gull, appearing suddenly almost above his oar, was silent and terrifying as a ghost. It stared at him, and then was gone.

The sound of the conch shell seemed further away. Sometimes it stopped for a little, while Belle got her breath again. Ken knew just how she looked, standing at the bow, her hair dank along her forehead and her cheeks puffed out, blowing. She was scared. She began by blowing too often and too hard.

And he was rowing too hard. Guess he was scared, too. But easy does it. Rowing hard like that wasn't getting him anywhere It seemed to be getting him further away. Fast.

Ken rested on his oars and shouted. He gave the loudest shout he could. Twice. And then he listened. There was no answering shout. He was too far away for them to hear him.

But he could still hear the conch shell, still hear its despairing toots though they were fainter. Sounded like Cliff had it now, maybe. But it was a long way off.

Very carefully, very slowly, stopping to listen after every two or three strokes of the oars, Ken tried to steal up on the sound. But all his care did him no more good than his former haste. Perhaps he was rowing in circles as they say men, lost in the woods, walk. Perhaps the little cold wind was at work, separating those bits of floating wood from one another.

For after a while, when he stopped rowing to listen, he could hear nothing. Nothing? He strained his senses. He *must* hear. Perhaps Cliff was resting. There was nothing to be afraid of. The sound would soon begin again. Just wait until Cliff caught his wind, that was all.

But though he waited, still he heard nothing, and he knew that someone was blowing the conch but he couldn't hear it. He turned the boat about, or at least he thought he did, and rowed desperately back in the direction from which he thought he had come. But with no landmarks to guide him, not even a sound now, he had no way of being sure of anything. Even the breeze came fitfully, and it certainly seemed to be veering.

Ken longed for the sound of the conch shell. So long as he had heard that, the thread which tied him to the *Pluribus* and Cliff and Belle held. But now it was snapped.

He was all alone on the sea, in a fog, in the smallest possible of boats. The pea-pod was a good little harbor boat, but never intended for anything else. Cliff always hauled her aboard the moment the least sea began to run.

"If I only knew where the shore was," Ken thought. But he didn't. He might row further and further out into the open sea and never know it until too late.

"If only this darn fog'd let up," he thought, but he knew it might last for days.

He had the fish, but raw fish didn't seem anything a boy could eat. And he was cold. He had gone off in hot weather. Jiminy, it felt icy now. The cold added to his forlorn misery. There was nothing that he could do but keep on rowing, enough so he wouldn't freeze anyhow. But he was getting tired.

It must be about two o'clock to judge by how hungry he felt. Would Cliff and Belle eat anything with him lost? No, he knew they wouldn't. They were hunting for him as hard as he was hunting for them. Any moment the good old *Pluribus* might loom up out of the fog, and he'd be handing Cliff the end of the painter and Belle'd be hugging him and maybe shaking him, too, after the scare she'd had! Gosh, a shaking would feel good in this fog.

Ken gave a kind of smile, but he felt a lot more like crying.

And still there was no sound of any kind, and the fog came in thicker and thicker until at last Ken, looking around at nothing, seemed to be the only living thing left in all the world.

Chapter Seven

~~~~~~

SOMETIMES the fog grew thinner and shone with the cold whiteness of an unseen sun; hope would spring again in Ken's heart and he would look eagerly about him and shout, but the only answer he ever had was the scream of a gull. Try as he would to pierce the white veils about him, he never saw the schooner nor any sign of land.

Then the heavier fogs would trail towards him, dragging along the surface of the sea, and the faint brightness would tarnish again to dull gray, and Ken would have to take up the oars, shivering with cold and discouragement.

Once, and only once, he thought he heard the far-off blare of the conch. But if he did—and he was not sure of it—it must have come on a flaw of the wind, for though he shouted until he was hoarse and listened, too, cupping his hands to his ears, he heard nothing more from the *E Pluribus Unum.*

Ken's situation was not a pleasant one. He had known of more than one man, carried in a dory out to sea on the tide in a fog, or after some mishap of the oars, who had been picked up, dead of exposure. There was Tom Haggett; he was the last one—married less than a year, and they didn't find him for three days, lying on top of the lobster traps in his boat.

The men he knew about had been lost in dories. But he was lost in a pea-pod, and his dangers were doubled. In any sea at all a pea-pod would founder. Not like a dory, which was so seaworthy that a man once rowed and sailed across the ocean in one, he'd heard his father say.

Thinking of home, the memory of the kitchen rose up before him, and of his mother taking a pan of gingerbread out of the oven, smoking hot, and of Emily, like as not doing his old job of setting the table, and his father and Ralph and Stuart, walking up from the shop, slapping the yellow sawdust off their clothes. It all seemed so warm and familiar. Ma's nasturtiums would be in bloom, and Emily probably would pick the seeds for pickles. When they heard about him, he hoped they wouldn't blame Cliff and Belle. He was the one who'd wanted to go fishing.

[66]

He had only himself to thank. Yet, whatever happened, he wasn't sorry he'd chosen to go to sea.

About the middle of the afternoon he heard the barking of seals coming out of the fog, and roused himself from the stupor which had come over him. Somewhere there were seal rocks and ledges, and

they were oftenest found off an island. He rowed very slowly along with the tide, in the direction in which the boat had been floating. This time his caution was rewarded. The sound grew louder and nearer. As a second blessing, the fog began to thin and silver, and suddenly he saw dimly the rocks and the wet gleam of the seals, lying on them like enormous sea-slugs. They were the first sight of any object outside the boat which he had seen for hours, since the seagull had flown by at the first coming of the fog.

Ken hoped there would be an island, or the mainland, not too far from the rocks. He must circle the ledges, keeping them in sight, praying that he would come upon land. To lose touch with the rocks and be swallowed up again into nothingness was too terrible to think of. He would begin by rowing in a fairly close circle around the seals; then, if he must, in wider and wider circles. He would not allow himself to think of what might happen if the circle became too wide.

Ken began to row across the tide, beginning his circle. The fog was thickening a little, coming in, tattered and formidable, but he could still see and hear the colony, and soon two heads appeared just beyond the stroke of his oar, and he saw that a mother and baby seal were watching him. They stared for a minute or two out of round dog-like eyes, and then disappeared.

Ken's luck was changing now. He heard a new sound, the lap of very small waves on rock. Then something stood dark and high in the fog, and it was a spruce-lined shore. Ken rowed along it, looking for a good place to land, and after a while he came upon a cove and an old fish house built on a shelf of rock. There had been a wharf, too, but it had fallen in.

Ken rowed the flat bow of the pea-pod onto the ledge and got out, stumbling with stiffness and exhaustion. He pulled the boat well up above high-water mark and looked about him. There might be people here, or there might not. Certainly the fish house had not been used for a long, long time.

The best thing he could do was to light a fire right away and get warm. Ever since he could remember he had carried matches, in one of his mother's preserve jars with a glass top. His father had taught him that when he showed him how to bait his first hook. The jar was in the old box under the stern seat.

Ken set about finding dry wood, or fairly dry wood. Nothing could be dry in this fog. But there was part of a broken lobster pot which would burn well, and driftwood, too, years out of the water. He made a heap of them in the shelter of the fish house, and then unsheathed his knife and made a small pile of dry shavings in the middle. The first match wouldn't burn. But the second did, and the third lighted the fire. He coaxed the flame carefully until the larger pieces caught.

Only then did Ken feel a measure of security. But he needed food as well as warmth. He returned to the boat, brought out the fish, and cleaned them. He did not want to wait for ashes, so he cut a green stick and cooked the largest fish over the flames. It was half burned and half cooked, but he ate it all and felt better.

He put the other fish on the roof of the shed, out of reach, he hoped, of prowling animals, looked again at the pea-pod, tying its painter to a nearby spruce for added security, put out the fire, took the matches with him in case he might get lost on the island, if it *were* indeed an island, and struck inland, following the remnant of an over-grown path.

He was warm now and fed, and there was a fair chance of his finding people sooner or later. Even if he didn't, he could probably make out for a while. But he wished the path showed some signs of having been used recently. He could see only ten or fifteen feet ahead of him, so he went slowly. First there was a stretch of spruce. He wouldn't lack for fuel.

Then the path came into a pasture, somewhat over-grown but still in use, for he could see recent signs of sheep. That might mean people, too, and then it might not.

He tried to establish landmarks at the beginning of the path into the spruce, studying the shapes of the boulders and snapping low twigs, leaving their ends hanging, to help him find the place again.

Then he crossed the pasture, noticing with satisfaction that there were plenty of blueberries, but not stopping now to gather any. There were field mushrooms, too. He knew them by their smooth cream-colored domes lined with pinkish brown gills. He came to a stone wall, higher than any he had ever seen and still in good condition. Beyond it was another stone wall, equally high, and a lane lay between. He turned and followed the land uphill. It had been used, but not much, and not by anything with wheels for many years, though the old ruts still showed.

Everything smelled of the sea, and the land seemed to slope down on either side of the lane. He could see old fields and new patches of spruce here and there. The place had an island feel to him, but it still might be the mainland. He couldn't see far enough to see water, but he felt it all about him, quiet under the fog. For once land under his shoes felt good. Emily herself couldn't have welcomed the stones and grass and spruces and blueberries more warmly than Ken did just then.

The lane, still accompanied by the two high walls, met a second lane, and, still climbing, Ken turned left. He was probably coming to the top of the island now, facing, like the round blunt head of a whale, into the sea. Some people built their houses on the head of an island, some down on the low part where the flukes of the whale would be. This looked like a one-house island to Ken, but he might be mistaken.

The lane came into another field, still surrounded by high walls. The sheep had been here, but not many of them. He walked on, following a path which looked more used.

And then out of the fog appeared the house. The front had fallen in. He could see the red-painted room downstairs and the big fireplace and the upstairs chambers under the pointed roof.

It was like some forlorn doll's house with one whole side left open. Certainly no one was living here. But when he came nearer, he saw that perhaps the place was still used, now and then as a cave might be.

Someone had built a bunk into one corner of the main room, and this was heaped with hay. There were ashes of this year's fires in the huge fireplace, and a few old pots and pans and a broiler stood on a shelf with two or three plates and a cracked mug and salt in a tin and several old-looking cans of food. The rotting floor had been patched by boards laid across the worst places, and someone had swept the fallen plaster from the ceiling into a corner, where it lay beside the worn butt of the broom which had swept it there.

Ruinous as it was, open along the entire front, except for an ell with four walls, with no roof, the old house still had a curiously compact and even cozy look. The chimney was enormous and made of very old, soft pinkish bricks. There was still an oven to be seen beside the wide fireplace, and the old plaster had been painted a soft Indian red, perhaps a hundred years ago. A wide doorstep of granite stood where a door had once been and along the stone Ken saw that there were johnny-jump-ups growing in the grass. Where the clapboards had come loose, he could see the sheathing of birch bark which had kept the house warm in winter.

Shell of a house though it was, it would do him until the fog lifted, as it did the owner of the sheep who must use it when he had occasion to come to the island. By now Ken was certain that he *was* on an island and that it was deserted, but, though people and hot food and a bed would have been very welcome, he still felt so grateful for solid land and now this shelter, that he was sure that he could take care of himself until help came.

"I'll just see about the well before I go back for

the fish," Ken thought. He had only gone halfway around the house when he came to a path which led in a few yards to the well. Here, again, a battered bucket, upended over a coil of rope, showed that the well was still in use.

"That's that," thought Ken with satisfaction. "Now for the fish."

But as he turned to retrace his steps he heard a lamb bleating down the pasture. It was the kind of bleat a lost lamb will give, and Ken unconsciously waited for the answering blat of the ewe. But there was no answer. Again came the bleating, and again Ken was surprised by the silence.

He shrugged. Lambs always find their mothers. This was no business of his. But suddenly an idea came to him. Although sheep had been pastured on the island, this was the first time he had heard any sound from one of them since his arrival. And that now struck him as odd.

Well, how often *did* sheep bleat? He'd probably hear plenty of them, when he went back to get the fish. Perhaps hearing him on the path had made them all keep still. It was time for him to get along.

Then the lamb bleated for the third time and for the third time there was no answer.

It was too much like the conch shell.

He'd have to see what was the trouble before he

went anywhere, and, a little exasperated with himself for wasting time on a wild goose chase, Ken started down the pasture into the fog.

Several times he was deceived by gray boulders which looked like sheep, but the lamb heard him coming and began bleating pitifully. It was not far off. He found it standing beside what was left of the carcass of a slaughtered sheep. And beyond that there were others. Perhaps a dozen in all. Someone had come to the island, and killed the sheep, and butchered the meat, and taken the best of it and the hides, leaving the rest lying about, a sickening sight. Ken felt his anger mounting. To go to an island and kill the sheep on it was one of the most despicable crimes a man could commit on the Maine coast, as bad as pulling another man's lobster pots.

Why had they left the lamb? He stared at the little thing standing by its mother's carcass, a late lamb by its looks.

It let itself be picked up, turning its round woolly head to look up into Ken's face, and Ken talked to it encouragingly.

"We'll make out, lamb," he said.

At least there were two castaways now.

~~~~~~

Chapter Eight

THE night set in as foggy as the day, without a ray of moon or star to lighten it. But by that time Ken was snug in the crumbling house.

The lamb wished to follow him about, but it got in his way, and after a little he shut it into the roofless ell and, in the deepening gray of a foggy twilight, hurried down the lane towards the cove. In the small visible circle in which he moved, he kept a sharp lookout for such landmarks as he could see and did not let himself think about the question of the killing of the sheep, knowing that he would need all his attention to guide him, with the fog still pressing in everywhere.

When he came to the first landmark, two stones set on one another on top of the wall to show where to cross into the pasture, he could hardly believe that he was already there, the path had seemed so much shorter on the second trip. In spite of the fog he scarcely had to hesitate for clues. As though walking in a cloud, he crossed the open land, found the marked spruces and the path, and came out on the cove and the small lapping of ripples. Something, whether bird or animal, had dragged one fish further along the roof and eaten half of it, but the others were untouched. Ken took a last look at the pea-pod, firmly tied, as he had left it, and pulled up under the bank, and with his fish in the bait basket, retraced his steps without difficulty, although it was almost dark by the time he reached the doorstep and the broken front of his shelter.

The lamb made a great baaing at his approach, and he opened the paneled door and let it join him, while he remade the fire and cooked himself another fish and heated a can of peas. He had no hesitation in using what he found on the old shelf, knowing that when in need, a stranger is welcome to whatever may be in a camp. When the store boat found him, he could replace anything he had used and more, too. But he would have to husband his resources. There were not many cans: coffee, condensed milk, a large can of baked beans, a can of tomatoes, and the peas which he had opened. But to-

morrow, if the fog held and there were still no chance of rescue, he would gather blueberries and mushrooms and blackberries.

When Ken had eaten, he washed his dish and fork and spoon and left them to dry by the fire. There was a lantern with oil in it hanging on a nail. He lighted it and went over to the bunk made of birch posts and a few boards. The man who had made it was no carpenter, but it would do.

Ken tossed up all the hay in the bed and found, as he expected, a mouse's nest, which he put, young mice and all, in a wisp of hay in the corner of the room. Now his preparations were all made. There was more hay in the ell, and he made a bed for the lamb and shut it up for the night. Then he turned the lantern down to a mere spark of light, and hung it back on the nail, and got into the hay, leaving on all his clothes, but taking off his shoes. From his bed he looked out across the old room to the fire burning low in the great worn fireplace. The dull red of the room glowed softly in the firelight; there was still glass in place in the small panes of the windows to the north on either side of a door, but to the south there was nothing but the night, with its white sheet of vapor which flowed, even into the room. The house was like a big lean-to, Ken thought. Or like a room on a stage.

He had only once been to the theatre, when the
gave *Uncle Tom's Cabin* at Rockland and the whol
family had hired a gig and driven over. They hadn'
got back until two o'clock in the morning. It wa
quite an expedition, but worth it, ten times over.

The side of the house lay all in pieces on th
ground where it had fallen. Ken figured it must hav
blown down in the big gale two years ago, which h
remembered because old Mr. Young had lost the roo
off a hen coop. Even half fallen down as it was, Ke
liked the place. He wondered who the first peopl
were who lived in it and built all those fine ston
walls.

A few hours ago he'd been drifting to sea in th
pea-pod, and here he was on land, with a roof ove
his head and a dinner inside him and a warm be
to sleep in. Never mind the musty smell. A smel
wouldn't hurt anyone.

Of course everything wasn't hunky-dory on the
island. Down the pasture were all those sheep car-
casses. That was an ugly business. But whoever had
killed them had taken what they wanted and gone.
There'd be no reason for them to stay around after
they'd done a thing like that, and good reason for
them to get out quick. Ken tried not to think about
it, and tired as he was, he soon went to sleep.

He was awakened some time in the night by hearing a man's voice at a little distance. It took him a moment to remember where he was. The fire was down to ashes and embers. The musty hay tickled his face. Then he remembered, and lay very still, listening.

He heard curses and then: "Where the devil is that lamb?"

Another voice, not so deep, said "Told you we ought to take it along."

The first voice cursed again.

"And have its blats giving us away? Here it was on the hoof until we'd sold the rest and could come back for it for ourselves."

"Well, t'ain't here now. Foxes may have took it."

"Too big. It's strayed somewhere. We'll find it."

While the men talked, Ken had slipped out of bed and put on his shoes. Looking out of the window he could see a faint light in the fog which he knew must be a lantern, not far off down the pasture, moving about as the men searched among the bushes. They were slowly working up towards the house. What should he do?

"Dad always says to carry the war into the enemy's country," Ken thought. "These men've been up to mischief and they'll be scary."

Working fast, he threw an armful of hay onto the embers so that the fire suddenly blazed and, catching the lantern from the nail, turned up the wick as far as possible and ran out of the north door, slamming it behind him. He made directly towards the other lantern, holding his own high and running as noisily as possible. He would have shouted, but he knew his boy's voice would give him away. The sheep killers must think that a man was running towards them.

For what seemed an interminable length of time, the fog-haloed lantern down the pasture remained immobile. It took all Ken's courage to keep him running towards it, but suddenly, with an exclamation and "Let's get out of here!" the light jerked, and the man who held it began to run, with the other behind him.

Of the actual men, Ken could see nothing but vague shadows in the fog. It was the misty light of the lantern which his lantern followed like vengeance. Once the foremost fugitive stumbled and nearly dashed out his light and Ken slowed down until the flight was renewed. He had no wish to overtake the fugitives, but only to keep them on the run. They must think that he was the angry owner of the sheep, unexpectedly returned to the island. So long as they thought that, they would keep on running.

They had come to trees now, here a thin line only; Ken went slowly through them to give the men more time. When he came to the open, the other lantern had been blown out. Though he could see nothing at all, he could hear water and the sound of a dory being rasped hastily down a stony beach, then the thud of boots on planking and the rattle of oars in oarlocks and, last, the sound of someone hastily rowing away.

"Main must be over there," Ken thought. "This is the other side of the island from where I landed."

He turned his lantern low and, holding it between himself and the men, started back, still careful to carry it at man's height. But it would take a good deal to make the sheep killers suspect that what had chased them off the island was only a thirteen-year-old boy. Ken was pretty sure they'd not try to come back again for the sake of any lamb which they hadn't been able to find anyway. Not now that they'd think the owner was on hand.

The trip back to the house was easy enough. Ken kept working his way slowly uphill through the pasture, and after a while he could see a dim fog-shrouded light from the windows of the old house. The flare of hay had burned out almost immediately, but there was still a last glow from the fire. He probably had been gone only eight or nine minutes, though it had seemed a good deal longer than that.

The lamb began to bleat as it heard Ken come in. "All right! All right!" he told it. "Hold your horses. I'm back. And we've got to go to sleep. It's the middle of the night still. Maybe by morning the wind will change and blow this fog out to sea again."

Chapter Nine

KEN had gone to sleep hoping that when he woke up he might look out on sunshine and a bright blue sea below his headland. But when he opened his eyes, it was to see the familiar fog, stretched like a curtain across the front of the room where he lay. Yet it was a moving curtain and thinner than it had been the day before. Wisps wandered about inside the house like faint inquisitive spirits, tiptoeing silently here and there, and melting away before the stare of the boy in the corner of the room.

Hearing him move, the lamb began calling from the ell, and Ken rose, a little stiffly, to let it out. There was hay in his hair, and he felt tired and listless after the hard rowing and the anxiety of the day before. He stood where the door had been and looked around him. The fog was certainly frazzling out. Now and then a spruce appeared in a rent of the veil, or a piece of the stone wall, or even an eye of blue sky, only to disappear again. But he could still see nothing of the shore.

After he had fried some baked beans in a pan and made some coffee, Ken felt better. He found a large bare shelf of rock and began gathering on it a heap of dead wood. Fortunately there was an axe in the house, and with it he lopped off the dead lower branches of the spruces and dragged them across the pasture until he had a high heap of them. Then he made a heap of green branches, for, when the time came for lighting a fire, he would want a great deal of smoke which would show up against the sky.

It was hard work, but Ken began to enjoy it. He imagined how Cliff and Belle would feel when they saw the signal and guessed that he was safe on shore. After he had finished the brush pile, he cut down a young spruce and lopped off all its branches until only a pole was left. Then he hunted about the house, going up the dangerous stairs to the upper storey and looking about the two little chambers there under the roof, but nowhere could he find a piece of white cloth, and ruefully, at last, he sacrificed his shirt, tying it to one end of the pole.

It was not easy to climb into another tree carrying the pole with him, but at last Ken succeeded, while the lamb stood below, watching his every move from its agate eyes. It had adopted him as its next of kin and hated to have him out of sight for a moment. When Ken had finished lashing the pole to the top of the spruce with a piece cut from the well rope, and climbed down out of the tree, the lamb greeted him with great delight.

The boy was touched by its devotion and played with it for a while, scratching its woolly head and pretending to push at it as another lamb might push. The creature was puzzled, but pleased, by the attention; and, when Ken went back to the house to build up the fire to cook the last of his fish and some more baked beans, the lamb followed him more closely than ever.

When the dishes were washed, Ken came out to the headland again. Now there was no doubt that the fog was trailing back to the sea from which it had come. He could make out whole stretches of the shore line below him and the blue water, radiant through the haze. Blue sky shone everywhere with the hurry of fog across it. There was scarcely a sound, but he had a sense of almost furtive movement on all sides.

Once more the fog was in full retreat.

As suddenly as it had come it was gone, drifting seaward and then melting entirely away. The sea lay below Ken's eyes, a vast sparkle of little crisscross waves, a plain of deepest blue. Several vessels appeared in sight, two or three of them schooners, and one tacking up the river he was sure must be the *Pluribus*. He was so excited that he scarcely glanced on his left where, not very far away, lay the shores of Deer Isle and the dark stubble of spruce woods outlining the green squares and oblongs of fields, with here and there a white pattern of little houses and barns. Later, he'd find on the chart where his island lay. Now all his attention was fixed on the store boat. How soon would Cliff and Belle see his signals? He'd soon know.

Ken looked up to his shirt, flying high over the spruce tree. Then he hurried into the house for dry hay and matches, with the lamb trotting after him.

Carefully he arranged his materials and lighted the dry wood and, as soon as the flames were crackling, began to lay on the green branches, until the smoke rose in a heavy twisting column, almost like a pillar.

The vessel he had taken for the *Pluribus* changed her course and made for the island.

"They've seen us!" Ken shouted to the bewildered lamb. "It's Cliff and Belle!"

He hurried into the house and made sure that all was in order. The dinner fire was out, but he scattered

the ashes and poured water on them. Then he lifted the mouse's nest back into the hay where he had found it, and closed the door into the ell. There was nothing more to do in the house.

Outside, his first glance went to the approaching schooner. It was still holding to its course in a light breeze. He climbed the spruce tree, lowered the pole, and regained his shirt. Then he scattered the remaining unused wood well below the outcrop of rock and began beating out the fire, bringing pail after pail of water from the well to throw on it. For a long time it seemed to fight back at him, spitting sparks and sending up great clouds of scalding steam and smoke at every onslaught of the water, but in the end he mastered it, until he could trample out the last wet embers with his shoes.

Even then Ken made very sure, looking everywhere for any smallest plume of smoke, either from the bed of the fire or from the ground beyond the rock, but in the end he was satisfied that the fire was out and would stay out. Then at last, with another quick look to make sure that the schooner was still on her course, he hurried back to the well and coiled the mended rope under the upended bucket.

"Come along, lamb, it's time to be going," he called. But it was unnecessary to urge the lamb, which had been following him back and forth from well to fire and from fire to well, uncomprehending, of course, but determined not to be left alone for a minute if it could help it.

Now it trotted at Ken's heels down the lane between the stone walls, which came as high as the boy's shoulder. At the trail marker Ken lifted the lamb over the wall. Under its coat of wool it was much lighter than it looked. Together they ran down the pasture and through the spruces. The water beyond was a dazzle of light and, like a vessel sailing through diamonds, the old *Pluribus* appeared, headed for the island.

Ken untied the pea-pod, shoved it down to the water, and lifted in the lamb which rolled its eyes for a little but stood still as Ken got in, pushed off, and settled to the oars.

He heard a joyous toot from Belle on the schooner, showing that he had been seen, and glancing over his shoulder, noticed that Cliff had changed his course a little so as to meet him. Ken's shoulders felt stiff from yesterday's long ordeal at the oars, but it seemed wonderful to him to be on the water again in the clear bright sea-smelling air, the planking of a boat under his feet and the lisp and lapping of waves all about him.

As the schooner came within shouting distance, Belle's voice hailed him. She seemed in no mood to scold. Pretty soon she began inquiring about the lamb, and it was she who leaned down over the rail to take it up when the pea-pod got within reach. The lamb, fortunately, held still while Ken, balanced with his feet wide apart on the thwart, handed it up to her.

Cliff, having brought the *Pluribus* into the wind, came up grinning, to give Ken a hand over the rail.

"See you brought dinner along," he remarked, clapping the boy on the shoulder. "Found folks on the island, did you? Didn't know as anyone was living on Star now."

Ken told them the whole story, while Cliff smoked his pipe and Belle knitted a sock, dropping half the stitches.

"I'll have to rip it all out later," she said, "but I'm so excited I've got to be doing something. There was times yesterday I wondered if we'd ever lay eyes on you again in this life. That signal smoke was about the most beautiful sight I ever saw."

As for the sheep butchering, both the Trasks were indignant.

"Dirty trick," said Cliff. "There's always scum wherever you go. They'll know at Stonington who the flock belonged to, and we'll notify him and replace the stuff you used."

Even Marigold was glad to see Ken back and very

curious about the lamb, although she skittered away
when the larger animal reached down an inquiring
nose towards her. Ken was going to make a halter
but Belle said, "Let it run loose. We'll be in at Stonington before night."

The pea-pod was taken again in tow, and the
storeboat, sailing before the wind, moved sedately
along the coast towards its next port of call, while
Belle and Ken began decking out the shrouds with
as much of the stock-in-trade as they could carry.

They came into Stonington in full regalia to find
a crowd, mostly of women and children, already at
the wharf to meet them. After the first rush of visiting
and shopping had begun to lull a little, Cliff said to

an acquaintance, "Wonder if you could tell me who owns Star Island now?"

"Man named Joel Green. Runs the grocery up the street."

"He keep sheep on the island?"

"Yes, I believe he does. A small flock nowadays. Hasn't lived there for better than twenty years."

"Guess I'll go see him. Want to come along, Ken? You be all right, Belle, while we're gone?"

"Don't hurry back. I can manage fine by myself," Belle said. In honor of being in port she had put on a dress over her trousers and boots, and a straw hat with a ribbon, and was now deep in gossip and salesmanship.

Cliff and Ken walked up the street past the stone quarries and came to the store where they found a middle-aged man, with a pleasant spectacled face, standing behind the counter.

"Anything I can do for you?" he asked, and Cliff said, "Mr. Green?"

"Yes, Joel Green's my name."

"I'm Cliff Trask off the store boat, and this is Ken Philbrook. His father builds sloops over Friendship way. Ken, you tell Mr. Green about what happened to you last night. First I'd better say Ken got separated from the *Pluribus* in the pea-pod during the fog yesterday. My wife and I was real anxious, but he made out to land on Star and spent the night in an old house he found there. Now, Ken, you tell the rest."

So Ken told the story of the butchered sheep and of the two men he had heard in the night, while Joel Green listened carefully, asking a question now and then.

At the end he said, "I guess that finishes my sheep raising. I've let the flock grow small. Didn't seem to have time for them. And I shan't buy any more. This takes it out of my hands."

"Who do you think'd do a thing like that?" Cliff asked.

"No one from around here. But a lot of strangers drift along the coast, especially in summer. I've heard of a man selling mutton to the quarry camps but didn't pay any heed. Now, like as not, he's skipped. I shan't try to do anything. Just be a waste of time, like hunting a flea on a St. Bernard dog."

"We want to pay for those cans the boy used."

Joel Green's gray eyes smiled behind his glasses.

"Not if I know it. I shan't be going back now. Those few things aren't worth bothering about."

"We'll bring the lamb."

"Let the boy have the lamb. I don't want it."

"But there's a lot of meat on a lamb."

"I can get all the meat I want without any trouble. You've behaved very neighborly, letting me know how things stood on the island. I'd like the boy to have the lamb. He's the one who's rescued it. Let him have it, then. It's nothing to me."

Ken was very pleased. It had never occurred to him that the lamb could be his. He'd like to take it back to Emily. A girl would like a pet lamb. But then he heard Cliff say, "I'm sure that's more than kind, Mr. Green. Fresh meat's always welcome on board. We get tired of fish and clams sometimes."

Chapter Ten

~~~~~~

BY THE time they got back to the *E Pluribus Unum,* everyone had gone home for lunch and Belle was in the cabin, making sandwiches and coffee, which she now brought up on deck.

"Done a good day's business this morning," she remarked. "They was keen on buying as black flies on biting. Find Mr. Green?"

"Yes," said Cliff. "He don't seem much put out. You'd almost say he was relieved. Wouldn't take anything for those two-three cans Ken used, and gave him the lamb into the bargain."

"Well, now, that was real generous. You pleased, Ken?"

Ken hadn't spoken since he came on board. The lamb had run up to him the moment he was over the rail, but he pushed it away and sat staring at nothing.

When Belle spoke to him he looked up, tried to smile, and then said with difficulty, "Sure."

Belle gave him a long look.

She handed Cliff another ham sandwich.

"I always notice," she said, "folks will stare at any critter, though their own houses and barns may be crowded with them. Now you take this morning. Every child and half the womenfolks were after that lamb and Marigold. You'd think they'd never seen lamb or kitten the way they act. You'd better build a pen, Cliff. That lamb will be real good for trade."

Ken was listening hard. Now he looked at Cliff to see what Cliff would say, but Belle never glanced at her husband. She stumped off to the cabin for more coffee. When she came back she began talking about other things.

"Three people asked for rolling pins this morning. We'd better have some in stock."

But Cliff was still thinking about lamb.

"I figured we'd butcher it and have some fresh meat, Belle."

Belle shrugged her shoulders.

"It's worth more for advertising," she said casually. "Not that I care. It's up to Ken to decide. It's his lamb, ain't it? What do you say, Ken? Rather have fresh meat?"

Ken said carefully, "Just as soon use it for advertising. I thought maybe Emily'd like it when we got back."

"There!" said Belle. "I'm glad Ken's willing to let us use it. It's all one to you, ain't it, Cliff? We took in a nice lot of money this morning. I'll go up street this afternoon and lay in some meat."

"All right with me," said Cliff, who was only obstinate when opposed. "Could take another cup of coffee, Belle, if the pot ain't empty."

Ken felt the lamb nudging his elbow, and this time he let it come close, sharing the bread of his sandwich with it. He saw Belle looking at him, her eyes smiling, though her tanned heavy-featured face was expressionless. Why, she'd talked that way to Cliff on purpose, so he could keep the lamb. Gosh, there wasn't anything he wouldn't do for Belle.

They put in a good three days at Stonington, during which the lamb acquired a pen and a name. Ken called it Star for the island. And Belle was right about Star's being a drawing card. All the children made for its pen like bees for sugar, and often Ken let the lamb out to play with them. While the children played, the mothers lingered, and while they lingered, their eyes lighted on new things they wanted to buy.

On the last afternoon Mrs. Green came aboard to

do some shopping and, while buying dress goods, introduced herself to Belle.

"Joel was pleased at the trouble Mr. Trask took to let him know right away about our sheep," she said. "What a lot of bad people there seem to be. I can't imagine anyone's doing a thing like that when I was a girl. Joel don't take it hard. But I feel kind of bad about it. Seems as if the sheep were the last tie we had with the island. Star was where I was born, you know. Joel was raised in Stonington. But my folks have lived on Star since Indian times."

"You don't say so!" said Belle. "Indian times was a long while ago. Ken, you'd better come here. This lady is Mrs. Joel Green, and Mrs. Green, this is Ken Philbrook who got on your island in the fog."

"I stayed in the old house, Mrs. Green. I, well, I kind of liked it. It was different from any house I ever saw before."

"It's falling down now," said Mrs. Green with a sigh. "Joel's too sociable to care for islands, and we only stayed there a couple of years after we were married. Since then it's been going to pieces fast, and the whole front blew down in that bad gale a few years ago. But it was a good house. They built strong in those days, and somehow kindly. That house has been in my family nearly two hundred years now, and not one of our children cares a straw about it, or the island either."

"Did anything happen in Indian times?" Ken prompted and Mrs. Green smiled.

"My ancestor, Nathan Stone, built it about 1690 and brought his wife to it and raised a young family. The Indians on Deer Isle didn't like having him there because he cleared so much land and drove off the seagulls. They'd been accustomed to coming out to Star every spring to gather seagulls' eggs. They complained and complained to Nathan, but he paid them no heed and just went on clearing."

Belle clucked her tongue sympathetically, and Mrs Green continued her tale.

"Then came on one of those French and Indian wars. Seemed like they got a-going every few years. And the Indians swarmed out in their canoes and went for Nathan. He saw them coming and hid in a big brush pile he had where he was clearing land. They took his wife, Polly, and four or five children captive, but they didn't find him, and, of course, Polly said he was off island. But his own dog gave him away, running round the brush pile and whining. Didn't mean harm, of course, but the Indians killed him before Polly's eyes and made off with everything they wanted in the house. I don't know why they didn't make out to burn it, but they didn't."

"And then?" urged Ken. He could imagine just how the Indians came—like fog—across the cleared land, and how the house looked and everything.

"I don't know much about it," Mrs. Green said. "Polly never came back. They were all taken to Quebec, and she married a Frenchman and turned Catholic. And I believe one of the girls ended up way across the ocean in France. But two of the boys got back to Star after the peace, and Nathan the Second stayed there and raised his family there. I've heard my father tell how, when the boys opened the door, they found, lying there in the middle of the floor, one of their father's shoebuckles an Indian had dropped. And they'd been gone upwards of ten years, I believe." Mrs. Green's voice changed and grew brisk.

"Now I've talked too long. When anyone shows an interest in Star I just let myself go, Joel says. But I miss the place, and that's the truth."

"I was only there a night," Ken said, "but I liked it better than any place I've ever seen."

Mrs. Green looked pleased. "Maybe when you're grown you'll come back and buy it. My children don't care for it. They take after Joel that way.

Even if the rest is pretty well gone there'll always be the chimney."

"And the stone walls," said Ken.

"And the walls," said Mrs. Green. "I always liked those walls. I never saw walls like those, here or any other place."

"I'll come back," said Ken.

Belle gave him a quick pat on the shoulder.

"When Ken says a thing, he means it," she told Mrs. Green. "Likely enough, you'll see a family on Star again before you know it."

"I'd be real pleased, I'm sure," said Mrs. Green. "And I think I'd better look at your pie plates before I go. Mine are getting real bunged-up."

Ken drifted away. But now he had two ambitions. One was to go to sea on his own vessel, and the other was to have his house on Star. He'd tell Emily about it this winter. It was all a long way off, but he saw the shape he wanted his life to take.

Chapter Eleven

~~~~~~

THE summer and fall were for Ken all that a summer and fall should be, and Belle and Cliff Trask said that they couldn't remember when they had had such a good season. Somehow, the three of them just suited each other, like cups and saucers you might say, and Marigold and Star fitted right in, too. After the first week the kitten and lamb got used to each other, and half the time Marigold would spend her leisure in Star's pen. In calm weather Star often had the run of the deck, and then she was always at Ken's heels, but Belle drew the line on her coming into the cabin.

"Out you go, silly!" she'd say, pushing the lamb good-humoredly with her broom. "No lambs below deck!"

Most of the weather was calm, though along in September they had some blows which gave Ken a chance to find out that he was a good sailor and never seasick for a moment. He loved the excitement of feeling the wild gusty wind off the Atlantic rushing upon them, while the good old *Pluribus* rolled and plunged under his feet.

"She ain't much for looks," said Cliff, "but the old *Pluribus* is a steady vessel, and never gives in. Why, I remember once Belle and me was caught in a sixty-mile gale off Monhegan. A lot of newer boats than the *Pluribus* was lost that night, but we come into harbor next day without so much as a sail blown away. The *E Pluribus Unum* was built sound as the currency of the United States."

"Yes," Belle agreed, "she's steady. There's never been a time I couldn't knit if I'd a mind to."

Ken was good aboard ship. He never lost his head and he never fumbled. At home in Friendship, somehow, he'd been different. Half asleep ashore. Only when he was fishing was he all alive as he was now. All alive and noticing. As he had been when he saw the dollar in the mud where Dale Fraser and young Dale had been digging clams. He used to remember that day sometimes, when he was polishing the lucky dollar, nailed back again in its place on the mast. That dollar had proved lucky for the schooner and lucky for him.

By fall he knew every port from Portsmouth to Calais, and knew a good many of the people in them, too, and what they wanted. It was nice being on a store boat. You had the sea, a whole lot of it, but then you had new people to get acquainted with all the time. Some places he had made such good friends with other boys that they'd asked him for dinner at their houses and to spend the night, and one boy, John Fossett, the Trasks invited on a cruise between harbors when he wanted to visit an uncle up Cherryfield way.

Three times during the summer the *Pluribus* put in at Friendship, and Ken had a chance to see his people.

"There's no doubt you were meant to go to sea," his mother said, looking at him closely the first time he came ashore. "You've grown an inch at least, and you look so brown, Ken! I can't even see the freckles. I'm glad I let you go."

If Ken looked well, so did Emily. She was like a little plant which had been too much transplanted and at last had a chance to put down its roots. Everyone made a lot of her. Even Ralph and Stuart acted glad to have her around, and Mr. Philbrook was nearly as devoted to her as his wife. The child had lost that wild look she had on the store boat. Ken gave her Star, and her eyes, blue and brown alike, shone with happiness over the present.

"When I'm gone she'll follow you, if you're the one who feeds her."

"Yes, but I like to have her follow you. If she didn't, I'd think she was ungrateful and then I shouldn't love her the way I do."

Emily took Ken down to see the pilot house of the *Thomas E. Bailey* under the pine. It was all re-painted. She said that Stuart had helped her with that. The place was neat as a fiddle, and she'd made a quilt for the cot herself, and a cushion for the old chair.

"Do you like it?" she asked anxiously, watching his face, and he *was* pleased, mostly that she had tried to please him, for after being at sea an old pilot house under a pine didn't interest him much, and this time he insisted on Emily's taking it for good.

If one wanted to like a *house,* he knew what the house would be, high up over the sea, and as old-feeling as a big boulder in the sun. He told Emily about Star Island, and she listened with her eyes wide and intent.

"Oh, Ken!" she said when he had finished. "I'd like to see that!"

"I'll take you there someday," he promised.

He was never home for more than two or three days at a time, and while the store boat was at Friendship, Emily used to go down to help Belle sell the dry goods. Now that they weren't together, they were quite fond of each other, and the Trasks were glad to have Emily around again.

"But when sail's hoisted, I'd a heap rather see Em'ly waving from the wharf," Belle declared. "Lands' sake, that child would go around like a wet hen. You wouldn't believe what a gloom one little girl could cast over a whole schooner."

"She was eating her heart out," said Cliff. "Look at her now! Merry as a grig."

"What is a grig, Cliff?" Ken asked.

"I don't know. Something that's merry is all I ever heard."

"It's a cricket," Belle declared.

"Can't prove it by me," said Cliff. "Merry, that's all."

It was good to be with the family, and Friendship looked a sightly place seen from the water, but Ken always felt a lifting of the heart when the *Pluribus* put out to sea again. Clear weather or foggy, hot and still, with the water like brass below, or chill and windy, stormy or smooth, Ken loved it all. He had learned his lesson. He did his fishing from deck, but he was never bored for a moment, even when becalmed. There were always things to do on the *Pluribus*, and when out of other employment he helped Belle knit heads for lobster pots or lighter nets for the glass balls the fishermen used for floaters, and he had started a model of the *Pluribus* which he worked at when he had a chance. There wasn't too much time between ports. He liked helping to trim up the store boat for her triumphal entry each time, and he enjoyed the welcome which always met them at the wharf.

Once at Bucksport they lay alongside a circus boat, and Ken was filled with interest. He went to the show twice and spent all his free time aboard the other schooner, helping to water and feed and bed down the animals. There were two or three monkeys and some trained dogs and a black bear and a gazelle from India and an old lion, which had lost most of his teeth, but could still roar. His name on the billboards was Scipio Africanus, and he was shown being captured by a dozen naked Negroes, with spears, looking very ferocious; but around the showboat everyone called him Skip and treated him pretty casually. One little monkey seemed to take a fancy to Ken and would jump on his shoulder and put a little arm tight about his neck.

"He don't do that to everyone," the showman's son assured Ken. "He bit a boy in Rockport, right through the thumb."

"Rather be on the circus boat?" Belle asked, a little jealously perhaps, the third evening when Ken came back to the *Pluribus* late for supper. But Ken, after considering, shook his head.

"It doesn't smell good," he said, "and when it's rough, Milton says half the animals are seasick."

"That so?" asked Belle. "Two years ago we lay alongside a showboat. That was at Camden, warn't it, Clifford?"

"Castine, I think."

"Well, I get confused. I know they was giving

Uncle Tom's Cabin and them bloodhounds kept me awake nights, baying."

"It was full moon, do you remember, Belle? Man who owned them said in the dark of the moon, they was mum as clams."

"If we meet up with them again I hope it will be in the dark of the moon then."

"I wonder if they were the ones gave *Uncle Tom's Cabin* at the Rockland Theatre the time Dad took us all to see it?"

"Might have been. When there was a theatre, they hired it. Otherwise they had a stage of their own, but not as large as they'd have liked, the lady told me."

Later on in August they heard that the showboat was touring the coast that season, but they never caught up with her somehow, though they did see the circus boat again for just a few hours before she left Bar Harbor, and the monkey acted as though it remembered Ken, and hung onto him with its little black hands and didn't want to let go.

Another time they met up with a doctor in a sloop jam crammed full of medicine he was selling up and down the coast. His best trade was in pulling out teeth, he told Cliff.

There was a rival store boat, too, new that season. They heard a good deal about her. Mostly people said she wasn't as well stocked as the *E Pluribus Unum,* but it was a little unsettling to have her working the same ports.

"I bet she's that one we heard about used to keep on the Massachusetts run," Belle said. "Don't you remember, Cliff? I think they used to call her the *Trader.* They told us about her down in Portsmouth three years ago. She'd been in there. But she's never come this far east before."

"I don't know why you think that this *Susan B.* schooner's the same as the *Trader,* but it may be for all I know. One thing I'm sure of, we'd better put in some more stock and, Belle, you'd best see if you can't pick up some fancy gewgaws to kind of catch the ladies' eyes. When you've got competition, you've got to smarten up your wares."

The presence of the *Susan B.* somewhere ahead of them, or behind them, added zest to the store boat's voyage, and in the end didn't seem to hurt trade. Maybe having two store boats coming in just kept people in a buying mood. Ken was always looking for a sight of their rival. There was a boy aboard about his age, people said, and one older, who sailed with their father. If they had a mother, she stayed home.

But Ken never had a glimpse of so much as the topsail of the *Susan B*. She remained as mysterious as the *Flying Dutchman* and she never even put into Friendship, so he could get no account of her from Emily and the family. There were lots of things to keep him interested. And among others he kept in mind the two men who had butchered the flock on Star Island. There had been something about the voices heard in the darkness which teased him by a certain familiarity. They sounded like people he knew, but he couldn't think just who they were. And most of the people he knew would be in Friendship, anyhow, not roaming around by night in a dory off Deer Isle.

Early in September Cliff stored the gardening and farm tools in the hold and brought out axes and snow shovels and pick axes and sleighbells. And Belle put away her cotton and gingham and percale dress lengths and showed wools and knitted scarves and shawls and long underwear, and buying, which had been easing off in August, perked up again.

Early as it was, everyone was talking about whether a hard or open winter was coming. Some went by brown and black caterpillars, some by squirrels' hoards, and some by the way the fish were acting; but no one agreed with anyone else.

"It's always a hard winter on the islands for the women, poor souls," said Belle. "They do feel so shut up. They can't go off island for five months on end. I've had my fling summers so I rather relish a quiet winter on Swan's, but I know how the rest of them feel."

Ken knew that the season was drawing to a close. The duck and geese were flying south now. He often heard them passing overhead. The fishermen complained that already the lobsters were going into deeper water off shore to keep warm. The boarding houses, on the points at the entrances to the harbors, had shutters over their windows now and looked out blindly to the sea, and one day a whole flock of big orange-and-black butterflies fluttered past the *Pluribus,* bright against the waves.

It didn't come as a shock to Ken when Cliff finally said, "Well, folks, I guess we'd better be leaving Ken at Friendship now, and going direct on to Swan's. Ain't enough money coming in to pay for the bother of sailing. It looks like it's time to get out our land legs for a spell of winter."

Chapter Twelve

~~~~~~

Mrs. PHILBROOK had asked the Trasks up for dinner on the night before they sailed, and the big table in the kitchen was crowded with people, three along each side and one at each end, with the big lamp in the middle, for the dark came early at the end of September.

Half the time Ma and Emily were out of their seats, waiting on table, smiling and proud because everyone ate so much of the good things they had been busy getting ready all day. The talk began with the store boat.

"Can't say as we had too bad a season," Cliff admitted, but Belle, for once in a regular dress and a pair of ladies' shoes, laughed one of her sudden hearty laughs.

"Cliff don't tell the half of it," she broke in. "In spite of another store boat on the run we took

in more over the counter than we've ever taken in. It was a lively summer from first to last."

Cliff grinned.

"Belle's boasting," he said. "But we didn't do too bad, and that's a fact. Ken's getting back the dollar kept things on even keel. He's been a first-rate help, and going to sea doesn't seem to have hurt him none."

Mrs. Philbrook smiled.

"It's done him good," she said. "I'll have to be getting him new clothes. He's grown out of everything he had."

Cliff went on casually, "Next summer Belle and I thought we could manage some wages, now Ken's learned the ropes."

Belle listened anxiously for the answer and so did Ken. Once again Mr. and Mrs. Philbrook's eyes consulted down the table and then Mr. Philbrook said, "We'll see when the time comes, but the likelihood is that he can go. If he can catch up on his school work, that is."

Ken relaxed. "Oh, I'll catch up."

"I'll help you," said Emily. "I'm in your grade and I've got all the books right here for you."

"Now you know all about us," said Cliff. "What about you, Otis? How's the yards?"

Just as Cliff had answered cautiously, so Mr. Philbrook said with apparent indifference, "Oh, we keep busy."

"Busy," repeated Stuart. "Dad should have said 'rushed.' And we've got the prettiest little sloop on the ways now we've ever had. Dad's been changing the design, and this one's a crackerjack. She'll outsail anything we ever built."

"And that's to say anything of the size anyone on the coast's building," said Cliff. "Doing her on order?"

"No," said Mr. Philbrook. "We're just going to see how she turns out."

"Dad means he can afford to ask his own price for her and wait till he gets it," Ralph said. "She's going to be a history-maker, all right."

"Tomorrow's Saturday," Ken volunteered. "I'll be down to help."

"Glad to have you, son," said Mr. Philbrook, but Ralph whistled derisively.

"The day you put in ten hours at the yards will be a day, Ken."

"You wait and see."

"Of course, he will," said Emily. "You don't know a thing about it, Ralph. When I couldn't be ashore I hated everything that sailed, and now I like to remember the *Pluribus* and all. And it's that way with Ken. He *had* to go to sea. Now he can go, he'll like the yards and being here winters. You wait and see."

Ken grinned. "I'd better learn something about building so I can help on my own sloop later on."

"When you're twenty-five," Ralph said.

For a moment Ken was taken in, but he saw the twinkle in Ralph's eyes and turned to Stuart.

"You promised when I was twenty-one, didn't you?"

"Sure thing." Stuart, who never was much of a hand at teasing, reassured him. "And if you help, it might be twenty. Mightn't it, Dad?"

Mr. Philbrook gave his quiet smile.

"Wouldn't say it mightn't be possible."

Belle laughed. "Don't be in too much of a hurry to leave us, Ken."

"Oh, I'm not. Only, of course, some day—"

"Sure," said Cliff. "Belle's only joking. So long as you don't run another store boat and cut into our trade."

"By the way," said Mrs. Philbrook, "the Frasers have turned up again, more out-at-the-elbows than ever."

"Bad pennies," commented Mr. Philbrook, finishing the last bite of pumpkin pie and wiping his mustache before he pushed back his chair a little from the table and lighted his pipe.

"Ought we to know the Frasers?" Belle asked.

"Sure," said Ken, "they were the ones robbed the *Pluribus* and went off with the lucky dollar."

"Of course! Now I remember. Surely the folks around here aren't going to let them stay?"

Mr. Philbrook took a long puff at his pipe and put in a little more tobacco from his pouch before answering.

"Well," he said slowly, "there's two ways to look at it. One's your way, Mrs. Trask. They certainly aren't desirable. But as Hector Young says, they've got to live somewhere. Can't take them out and drown them, and it don't seem neighborly to force them on other people. So Hector's going to let them use his old fish house same as he did before, and I expect some of my potatoes and parsnips will disappear same as they did. Of course, Carl Vinal means to keep an eye on them. Went down and told them so. We figure it's the best we can do, but that's not to say we wouldn't a whole lot rather never set eyes on them again."

Mrs. Philbrook was carrying dishes to the sink, but now she stopped with her hands full of plates and turned around.

"You know, I say half the trouble is they're not wanted anywhere. They've got that look of failure. Kind of lost hope. They try this and they try that and never get anywhere. You know how cats are who haven't a home and have gone wild? If someone would stake those two and they could get ahead they'd be all right."

"Ma says that because she saw young Dale take a thorn out of Ella Small's dog's paw once," said Mr. Philbrook.

"I've seen more than that," declared Mrs. Philbrook stoutly. "And what's more, I'm sending them down some clothes by Ken tomorrow."

"Ouch!" cried Ralph. "Don't you take any of my things without my knowing, Ma! Last spring you sent off my favorite work pants."

"High time you used another pair," said his mother, calmly turning back to her work, where, in spite of her protests, Belle, as well as Emily, joined her, while the men and boys sat at ease around the table, talking.

Ken had a fine evening. It was like a knot joining his summer with his winter. But when he said good-by to Cliff and Belle he didn't feel too badly. The store boat was going into winter quarters at Swan's Island, and late in May she'd be stopping for Ken on her first cruise down to Boston for supplies.

"It takes a little warm weather to thaw people out and make them ready to spend," Cliff explained. "We used to start soon after the ice was out, but it wasn't worth the trouble. We won't interrupt school too early."

Belle kissed both children.

"I'm so pleased you found a good home, Em'ly," she said to the little girl, and Emily leaned up and whispered breathlessly in her ear.

"They've started papers to *adopt* me."

"My, ain't that nice?" asked Belle warmly. "Who'd have guessed how things was going to turn out?"

The next morning, Ken was all ready to get to work at the yards, but his mother asked him first to take the things down to the Frasers.

Mr. Philbrook and the boys had gone over the bundle grudgingly, trying to rescue favorite old clothes which were being given away, but Mrs. Philbrook held firm.

"Just start wearing something else steady. It'll soon be comfortable. Land's sakes, you've got plenty of old things left! You won't be bare-naked," and, ignoring their pleas, she did up the bundle again and handed it to Ken.

"Can't I take it down this evening, Ma?"

"No. The sooner they get something decent on their backs the better. It won't take ten minutes."

"You'd better do what your ma says," said Mr.

Philbrook. "There's no arguing with her when she's got good works in mind," and he gave Mrs. Philbrook a look at once affectionate and rueful.

Ken took up the bundle and started down the slope towards the edge of the harbor. Emily waved to him from the window over the sink. He knew she wanted to come, but she had her work to do and didn't suggest it.

The *E Pluribus Unum* was already gone and out of sight beyond the islands but there were a lot of fishing boats at anchor and among them five or six of his father's sloops. Ken recognized every one of them by something in their line which only his father knew how to put there.

He wondered what the new boat would be like. Stuart said she was a crackerjack, and the Philbrooks, as a family, weren't given to praising their own work.

It occurred to Ken that maybe with a little practice he could learn to do scroll work for her bow. He'd found out this summer that he was good at whittling and carving. A crackerjack, like the new sloop was going to be, ought to have a little gold, curling back from her bowsprit, and that was something neither Dad nor the boys was any hand at.

Excited by the possibility, Ken loped along the

path through the fields, hardly thinking of his errand at all. He found the Frasers digging clams, and looking thinner and raggeder than ever.

At his hail they waded back to shore, eyeing him suspiciously all the time, and he suddenly wondered if they knew that it was he who had found the twisted dollar from the *Pluribus* in the mud where they had been digging, and thus had brought suspicion upon them.

He handed big Dale the bundle a little awkwardly.

"Hello, Mr. Fraser," he said. "Ma thought maybe you could use these."

"Thanks," said the clam digger. "Guess so. You back again?"

The words were simple enough but they set Ken's heart racing, and he turned his face away quickly so that the man shouldn't see his eyes.

"Yes," he mumbled. "Hello, Dale. Guess I've got to be going," and he hurried off without another word to either of them, leaving them staring after him.

For now he realized why the voices of the sheep killers, which he had heard in the night at Star Island, had sounded familiar. He was as sure as he was that the sun was shining, that, father and son, the Frasers had been on the island that night. Twice

now he had come upon the evidences of their law-
lessness.

With a shiver Ken wondered if there were to be
a third time.

Chapter Thirteen

MONDAY morning Miss Benson looked at Ken over the tops of her glasses, and a smile appeared among the long wrinkles of her face.

"Glad to see you're back, Kenneth," she said. "Home is the sailor, home from the sea. Had a good time? Most good times have to be paid for, and you'll have to pay for this with make-up work. But we'll get it over quickly. Hard and fast, as they say."

Ken had studied under Miss Benson since he was in the fourth grade, and he liked her. It seemed nice to be back in the schoolhouse he knew so well with all the other boys and girls whom he had grown up with. For several days he was quite a hero, and everyone wanted to hear about life on the store boat and his adventure on Star Island. They knew Star already. She was always tagging around after Emily when she got a chance. One thing Ken told nobody, not even his father or mother. Not even Emily. And that was about the voices he had heard that night, about their being the Frasers' voices. He didn't quite know himself why he didn't tell. Perhaps he didn't want to hear his father ask, "Are you sure, Ken? You could easy be mistaken in the dark like that."

Maybe you could easy be mistaken, but inside himself he was sure.

After the first two weeks, when it was study study all the time, he got a chance to get down to the shop. The first Saturday that he went down with his father and the boys after early breakfast, Ralph asked him, "Inspection trip?"

"Maybe," said Ken, not getting mad.

He knew well enough how to make himself useful in the shed, and now for the first time he enjoyed it. The smell of clean wood, the sound of hammers, the occasional speech of the men, all heard and seen in the shadows against the bright ripples of the harbor, and the scream of the gulls where the building stood open, made his work of cleaning up shavings and bringing tools and such things pleasant.

Stuart stopped on the floor beside him to look up at the sloop's hull, which was still half frame. "Can you see what a little beauty she's going to be?"

And suddenly Ken saw how she was different from all the other sloops his father had built. Somewhere, watching the gulls, brooding over fish, shading his eyes to study a porpoise in action, Dad had got a new idea, something maybe no one else in all the world had ever had. And standing there beside Stuart, looking up at the first beginnings of the vessel, Ken shared something of his older brother's pride and excitement.

Late in the afternoon Ken found time to go off by himself a little with a piece of smooth board and some chalk he'd found. Looking at the hull, he began drawing a pattern, like a branch with leaves on it, for the scroll. But it wasn't what he wanted. The leaves kept sticking stiffly up from the stem, however he drew them, and there were too many of them. He was absorbed in the problem, frowning and biting his lip, erasing with his elbow nearly as fast as he drew.

He jumped when he heard his father's voice behind him.

"I've seen worse. But maybe you'd better go down look at Si Smith's schooner. She's got some pretty trim. And when you've looked at her and Ben Hascomb's, pick a couple of young apple shoots and study them. Hold them butt end to the wind so the leaves ripple back. You always have to think of wind when you think of a vessel."

Ken went down to the harbor and when he'd seen Si Smith's *Adventurer* he thought he knew what was wrong with his own drawing and came hurrying back to draw again. He didn't like to have Ralph think he wasn't putting in a full day's work.

But still the leaves didn't look just right, and again he heard his father's voice. "You been to the orchard?"

"No, Dad. I thought after seeing the *Adventurer* I had the idea."

"Don't be in such a tarnation hurry. When you're making anything, look at what other folks have made, but then go back and see what God's made. And after that take time to ponder. There, Stuart needs help with that sheathing. Leave this until next week, and let it come clear in your mind."

"That's the way you do, Dad?"

Mr. Philbrook smiled.

"The idea for this sloop's been kind of simmering on the back of the stove for two years."

"Gosh."

Ken climbed the scaffolding with a new understanding of his father. He began to feel the excitement of shipbuilding, an excitement tempered by great patience. He even got so far as to ask Stuart if he really liked the work.

"Wouldn't change for any other job I ever heard of."

"Not even to be a captain?"

"Captain? Most anyone can be a captain, but it takes brains to build real good boats."

Ken was unshaken.

"I'd rather be a captain."

"No harm in that," said Stuart tolerantly, going on with his hammering.

It was a month before Ken had the scroll drawn to suit him, and then in his spare time he worked at it, learning the hard way, by himself, how to carve the pattern into the wood. Sometimes Emily and Star came down to watch him for a little, but Mr. Philbrook didn't encourage girls or lambs about the shop and soon shooed them off.

But on other days Ken and Emily were a good deal together. She was always ready to go with him, fishing or picking chestnuts or gathering apples from the trees back of the house, and often lent him a hand with the stove wood. And she relied on him in return. When Jim Bancroft, always a bully, teased her about her eyes being different colors and threatened to tie her braids to a nail on the schoolhouse door she told him, "You better not let Ken Philbrook catch you doing it!" and Ken, hearing his name, came right up and put an end to Jim's teasing. Emily was the only one in the family, except his father, who knew all the ports that Ken had been to. And his father hadn't visited them for years and, of course, had never laid eyes on the children. But Emily knew the children, too, and had

her own opinion of each, and she knew just how the harbors looked and what color the houses were painted. The two would sit by the hour, discussing the coast of Maine.

And while life went on, busily and quietly, the red-and-yellow leaves drifted from the trees, and the frosts came, and the ground hardened underfoot, and the children were glad to wear coats and mittens to school.

And then came the snow, uncertainly at first, staying only a few hours, and then a few days, and at last settling in and making itself at home for the winter. Ken and Emily were too old to build snowmen, but they made a fort and held it against all comers. And Ken got out his old sled, and they went sliding with the other children, screaming with excitement as they tore down the slope from the village, shot into the air over the bank at the shore, and landed on the harbor ice, with a satisfying bang, only to fly on, almost out to the islands.

Work at the shop slowed down, though they kept the big barrel wood-stove going and closed up the open front of the building. But even so, a man's hands were half numbed and everything took longer. By now the sloop was taking shape and finish; she would be ready for launching as soon as the ice was out. Ken's carving was finished, and Emily was helping him lay on the gold leaf, working at the kitchen table.

It was on a Saturday morning in early March when Mr. Philbrook looked up from his big plate of ham and eggs one morning to say, "I'm driving up to Waldoboro for a keg of nails. You two young ones want to come along?"

"I wish you'd asked me," Ralph spoke up. "Mil Davis said I could use his smelt shanty any time I liked, and Ma could use some smelt, couldn't you, Ma?"

"Indeed I could," said Mrs. Philbrook. "This time of year they taste good. But isn't it late? After this warm spell ice must be almost ready to go out."

"No. Everyone's still fishing. Ice is getting a little rotten but nothing too bad, the boys say."

"Couldn't Emily and I stop off and fish while you were in town, Dad?" Ken asked.

Mrs. Philbrook looked up, ready to object, but then she stopped. She let her husband decide for the boys what was safe or not safe. Her world was in the house, and there she gave the orders.

Mr. Philbrook considered.

"Bring your lines and bait anyhow and we'll see when we get there. Perhaps you'd better run over make sure Mil won't be using his house today."

The snow was thinning along the roads, but there was still enough for the livery sleigh and the bells rang out gaily along the phils as they started out. It was a fine day with a blue sky, and the white clouds had a springtime look, and the bluejays seemed very much in evidence.

"About time to be sugaring up country," Mr. Philbrook remarked. "Won't be much more winter now."

Their road took them along the broad Medomak River, and pretty soon they began seeing small groups of smelt shanties on the ice, with smoke coming from most of their stovepipes. They were made of canvas nailed on light frames and painted, some red, some brown, some green and some blue, according to their owners' fancies or the paint they happened to have in the shed. Set down as they were in a line, they looked like little village streets.

"See, Dad!" Ken exclaimed. "Everyone's fishing."

Mr. Philbrook nodded but said nothing. When they could see the church steeples of Waldoboro they came to a bend of the road, and another village of six or seven shanties well out on the ice.

"That's Mil's over there, the red one," urged Ken.

"We'll be careful," Emily chimed in.

Mr. Philbrook drew rein and for a long minute looked off over the river. The shanties were well out from shore above the current where the fish were running. There was smoke coming from three stovepipes.

"I guess it's all right," he said at last, not quite at ease. "I'll only be gone an hour or two. If you children hear the ice get to cracking, come right ashore as fast as you can and don't wait for anything. But folks seem to think the ice'll hold a while longer."

Emily and Ken climbed out, Ken with a basket of wood, split small and fine, and Emily with the bucket holding the lines and bait and a package of sandwiches.

Cheerfully waving their red mittens, they watched Mr. Philbrook drive off.

"I'll walk out and get you," he promised. "Inside, you couldn't hear me holler from the road."

In high spirits the children ran down the steep path to the shore. There was a path across the ice, too, easy to follow, but a little soft underfoot.

"It must be all right or people wouldn't be fishing," Emily said.

Ken agreed.

"There's Dale Fraser over there. Wonder who lent them a shanty?"

"Probably stole it," said Emily cheerfully.

"Dad says they haven't spunk enough to do anything that could be pinned on them. He says they're cowards, like stray dogs."

"I always feel awfully sorry for stray dogs," said Emily with sudden seriousness.

They waved to young Dale, who gave them an almost invisible nod as he went back into the smelt house. He was surly with everyone, worse even than old Dale.

When they glanced into the next house where a stove was going they found nobody there, though they could see clearly the marks of a pail and a pair of boots in the ice. Even the fire was almost out.

And the other shanty, which had seemed occupied, was empty, too. Ken looked at Emily a little doubtfully.

"What do you think?"

"Well, there's no house to go to. We'd freeze waiting around. We've got to light the stove and get in where it's warm."

Ken nodded slowly.

"The Frasers are out," he said. "Still—"

"Want to walk to Waldoboro?" Emily asked. "We'll be all right. It's only for an hour or two."

"Wish the shanty was nearer shore. It's out beyond any of the others."

"Could we move it?"

"Sure, but if we went in over the flats there'd be no fishing."

"Let's not worry then. Your dad wouldn't have said we could if there'd been any danger. Do light the fire, Ken. The wind's chilly in spite of the sun."

The inside of the smelt shanty was tiny, with

4. + D. H.

room for a very small stove, an old kitchen chair with a broken back, and a hole in the ice which seemed to lead down into a bottomless black pit.

Ken lighted the fire and baited the hooks for both their lines and each sat on half the chair. The little room filled with a cheerful warmth and soon they opened their coats. The outside world was all shut off from them by the canvas walls of their shelter. They kept very still now, for if they talked the smelt would not come near.

"I must listen for the ice," Ken thought. "I mustn't get too interested in fishing." But that was before the smelt began to bite.

Chapter Fourteen

~~~~~~

THAT'S funny. Didn't you feel the ice move?"
Emily asked, in a low whisper.

"It just goes up and down with the tide," Ken
whispered back, pulling in one of his lines.

"This didn't feel like that."

"I'll go and look."

But just then there was a tug on another of his
lines and Ken forgot what he was going to do.

About that time Emily had a rush of smelts,
the largest she had had that morning. She, too,
caught the fishing fever and forgot everything else.
If there were noises around them, the children inside
the little shanty didn't hear them. Their pail was
filling fast with small slim fish, drawn up through
the strange little window in the ice, with the cold
wonder of the sea still on their shining scales.

It must have been half an hour later, when the
run had paused again, that Emily joggled Ken's

elbow and whispered, "It seems to be moving *sideways*."

"What? Whisper louder."

"It seems to be moving *sideways*."

"What's moving sideways?"

"The ice."

"Oh!"

This time Ken got up, stiff from sitting so long on half a chair, and went rather casually towards the canvas door of the shanty, stopping first to put another small stick or two into the old stove.

"There! Feel that?" Emily asked, rather nervously this time, and forgetting to whisper.

This time Ken *did* notice a jar all through the ice under their feet, and with it went a loud groan.

He lost his casualness and put his shoulder to the door so hastily that he felt the canvas rip. Then it opened under his hand and he stood outside, with Emily crowding after him. The air felt cold after the heat inside, but the sun almost blinded them, used as they were to shadow. For half a minute they couldn't see what had happened, then Emily wailed, "We're adrift!"

A crack had appeared between them and the shore, and this crack had widened until it was three or four feet from ice to ice.

Ken pulled Emily forward.

"Could you jump that if you ran? I'd go over first and catch hold of your hands."

"Oh, I couldn't," sobbed Emily and even as she spoke the crack widened by another foot and Ken knew that neither of them could jump it now. If only he had paid attention to Emily when she first spoke! A board might still do. But there was no board. He began hauling desperately at the shanty stovepipe.

"Pull it over for a bridge—the canvas will hold us," he shouted, but again he was too late. By the time they had disconnected the pipe and lifted the shanty over the stove and hauled it to the crack, the blue-black water, pouring seaward, was too wide to be bridged, even by the frail bridge of canvas.

Emily was crying but Ken began to shout, "Dale! Dale! Dale Fraser! Help! Help! Help!"

Where the Frasers were, much nearer the shore, the ice had not yet cracked and there was no sign that the two had become alarmed. But at Ken's cries the door opened, and the man and boy stumbled out and stood, shading their eyes against the sun.

"What's the matter?" big Dale shouted.

"We're adrift!" Ken shouted back. "Adrift!"

Without another word the clam digger began to run heavily, in his big worn-out boots, towards them, with his boy after him.

When he got to the edge of the ice he stopped to look things over, with young Dale at his shoulder.

"Know anyone got a boat round here? Tide's going out." Even as he spoke the big floe on which the children stood was moving downriver. Sometime during the last hour or so the ice had given way, and now the part that felt the force was breaking off in larger or smaller pieces and floating down with the river. Their floe was about half the size of a barn floor. It tilted and turned a very little as it moved, but it was steady enough.

Ken gave a quick look at the riverbank, with its woods and cleared fields. A little down the road he could see Si Holbrook's house, but Si was old. He wouldn't be likely to have a boat in commission. And beyond him lived the two Dailey sisters. No help there.

"Gosh, no. Maybe Sam Hinks. But he's three miles down."

After the first moment of fright, Emily had stopped sobbing.

"Shall we swim?" she asked fearfully.

Fraser shook his head.

"No, you sit tight. We'll find something. Floe may drift in."

He and young Dale were walking along to keep

pace with the children's floe. But it didn't drift in. It was drifting out.

The man made a decision.

"Tear off that there door'n see if you can't steer her a mite towards the point. We'll try to meet you there," and, followed by young Dale, he started running again, back towards their shanty.

When Ken got to their own smelt house, lying on its side where they had left it, Emily was already trying to wrench the canvas door from the frame. Together they managed it, and together they held the awkward oblong in the river, trying to steady it between their bodies. It was very hard to do. Time and again the end they held almost swept them into the swift water as they felt the force of some strong eddy. The great awkward floe seemed almost uninfluenced by the frail rudder they were trying to use.

"Its no good," Ken panted at last, but Emily was more patient.

"At least we're doing *something*," she said. "And look, Ken, we're not going out as far as a lot of the ice. A piece passed us just a moment ago."

"My hands are getting numb."

"Maybe I can hold on alone. The stove's still going."

All alone on the ice, with the chair beside it, the stove stood, its stovepipe askew, with the smoke still coming out of it and a little pile of unburned wood in the basket beside it. At any other time Ken would have laughed, but, especially with Emily along, this being carried out on a floe was no laughing matter. He wouldn't leave the rudder, of course. With his weight gone, next thing they'd know, Emily'd be in the river.

He looked landward and there were the Frasers on shore, chopping down a young tree. Well, they must have some reason for it. He hoped they had time enough, that was all.

They seemed so slow he couldn't bear to watch them and looked away. If he'd been in a boat, he'd say the river certainly looked fine, such blue water with ice like big flat suds streaming out on it.

Just then another floe struck them, knocking off a piece of each of the ice rafts, and grinding along beside them for a little way.

"They're running along shore now," reported Emily.

Ken looked across to the still unbroken ice, along which, near the bank, he could see two rather small figures running, carrying a pole between them. Awkward as they looked, they were gaining a little on the floe. While he watched, they came abreast the

children, and then forged a little ahead. He hadn't
thought they were such good runners.

"They're going to get to the point before us,"
said Emily. "Push hard, Ken, see if we can't make
this old floe point inshore."

But push as they could and push as they would
on the door, the cake seemed to take very nearly its
own course, majestically sailing down the river.

The Frasers had reached the point, cutting across
the ice to its very tip.

"Goodness!" Emily said with sudden shrillness. "They're on a cake of ice, too!"

But the Frasers knew what they were doing. They had jumped on a small pan which they were poling towards the children. The water was shallow here; at low tide these would be flats. Big Dale had the pole and was working frantically. At last he thrust it into his son's hands, wiping his arm across his forehead.

The two floes were getting nearer. Emily and Ken could see the men's faces now, and even hear them panting. But the water was getting deeper, and the pan of ice moved more slowly now, as the poling grew more difficult. In spite of the now desperate efforts of the children to swing their floe inshore, or to delay it, they could see that they were in danger of sweeping past the Frasers. Nothing they could do seemed to help.

With a curse, big Dale snatched the pole out of his son's hands and, running to the very edge of his floe until it tilted sharply with his weight, he held the stick towards the children.

"Let go," Ken shouted to Emily and both children jumped clear of the door and ran towards the pole. But it was just beyond their reach. Ken's fingers brushed it, but he could get no hold. The floe, still in the current, swept past and out of reach.

Emily gave a shrill cry.

But young Dale was kneeling on the very edge of the ice now and had picked up a piece of board such as the fishermen, when fishing in the shanties, often put in front of their chairs to keep their feet off the ice. He was paddling, with every stroke dipping one mittened hand into the water. On the other side, Big Dale was poling, only now and then hitting bottom, but grimly doing what he could.

The space between the ice floes lessened, and suddenly, with a jar, the two came together. While young Dale continued his heavy paddling, his father came forward with the pole, and Ken and Emily grabbed the other end. It seemed like heaven itself to feel the hard wood in their hands.

"What d'you think, Pa? Try the big one?"

"Couldn't move it with that board. Kids had better come aboard this one."

"Hold them?"

"Might."

The man looked at the children.

"Girl first. Hop," he ordered Emily. Emily hopped, and the pan jarred under her weight, sending out a splash of water. Then Ken jumped, holding onto the pole until the last minute. They were all four on the small ice cake now, and the water looked very near.

But young Dale, his face streaming with sweat, was paddling again. He had scarcely given them a grin, but now he said, "One of you wipe my forehead. Can't see," and Emily, who was nearest, took the corner of her scarf and kept the sweat from running into his eyes. Pretty soon big Dale began to pole again and after that they moved faster.

They were being carried below the point, but all the time the water was shallowing and the tilting crazy little boat of ice was moving in towards the shore. And just before it touched solid ice, there was a shout from the road above them.

Mr. Philbrook, in the sleigh, had arrived in time to see the end of the adventure.

Chapter Fifteen

SOMEHOW, before they reached the shore, Mr. Philbrook had arrived. He helped Emily and Ken onto the solid ice without a word. It was to Dale Fraser that he spoke.

"I'm afraid the children have given you a lot of trouble," he said, shaking hands with the older man and then with young Dale.

Old Dale said, "Couldn't let them go out to sea."

Young Dale just grinned while he pulled off his wet mittens and began beating his hands across his chest.

"You're wet," Mr. Philbrook said quickly. "Won't you drive home in the cutter with us?"

Old Dale shook his head.

Young Dale said, " We got the stove going in the shanty. We'll dry out easy."

Without another word the two turned to trudge back to where the rest of the smelt village still stood on the big shelf of solid ice.

Emily ran after them, and they stopped rather unwillingly while she thanked them. Ken, too, shook hands and stumbled over his words. He was a little bewildered by realizing how much he owed to the Frasers.

"Be home this evening?" Mr. Philbrook called to old Dale. "Something I'd like to talk over with you."

The man gave a grunt of assent and this time walked off without turning his head again, though young Dale gave a quick half-wave of a hand before following him.

"Guess you didn't listen very hard," Mr. Philbrook remarked to the children as they climbed the slope towards the road. "There's always a lot of cracking before ice breaks off."

"We were fishing," Ken said.

"Yes," Mr. Philbrook assented. "I know how it is. I oughtn't to have let you go in the first place."

"Dad's pretty calm about it all," Ken thought until he reached the sleigh. There stood Major, the livery sorrel, his plush winter coat matted with sweat and his sides still heaving.

Emily, who hadn't spoken before, looked at the horse, and slipped her hand into Mr. Philbrook's.

"You must have seen us quite a ways down the road," she said, and then added shyly, "Dad."

With an air of surprise Mr. Philbrook stroked his long mustache, looked at Major and remarked, "That horse must have been running." Then the three climbed into the sleigh. Dad had plenty of feelings, the children could see now. He just didn't think there was any use in talking about them. But as they drove along slowly, so that Major could get his wind, he asked all about what had happened before he came on the scene, and Emily and Ken told him from the very beginning.

"I thought there wasn't much use hollering to the Frasers, Dad," Ken explained. "I remembered what you'd always said about how that kind is yellow."

"I was mistaken," Mr. Philbrook admitted. "It teaches me not to sit in judgment."

That evening after supper Mr. Philbrook lighted his lantern and went off to Mr. Young's fish house to have a talk with the Frasers. He was gone for two hours or more, and the family went to bed before he got back, leaving the lamp turned low on the kitchen table.

Next morning he remarked at breakfast, "I'm going to keep the new sloop. I've arranged with Dale Fraser to let him and young Dale take it out. We're to go shares on the profits."

There was a stunned silence, and then Ralph exclaimed, "Keep it and go into partnership with anyone you like, Dad, except the Frasers! They'll ruin her inside a month. It's like giving the cat a silver dish to drink milk out of."

Mr. Philbrook nodded. "Maybe you're right and maybe you're wrong, Ralph. But I've made the agreement. I thought I had the Frasers all pigeonholed, my own self. And I was wrong. Ma's always held they'd be all right if they could get back their self-respect, and if anything could give a fisherman his self-respect, it'd be to go out in a sloop like this last one."

Ralph put his face in his hands. "Scroll work and all," he groaned.

"She was the first of the type," said Stuart. "We'll never build another quite so good."

Ma Philbrook spoke up from her end of the table. "Then it's right and proper she should be used for a good purpose. If Dad goes halves with them, maybe he'll do better in the long run than selling outright. Ty Andrews used to send out half the boats he built on that arrangement, and it worked out good. Anyway, people are more important than things. If the Frasers can be helped back, a sloop couldn't be put to a better use, and there's no reason why Dad shouldn't do very well by her, too."

"You're right, Ma. It's just our sinful pride," said Stuart with a short laugh. "Come on, Ralph, let's do the thing up brown. I've got an outfit I could let one of them have, and you've got another. If they're going to go out in our new sloop, they've got to look halfways decent when they're on her."

How strange everything was! Ken had felt sure that there would be a third meeting with the Frasers, but he had never guessed how different it would be from the others! And he was glad he hadn't told anyone his suspicions about the men on Star Island. Now they would have their chance. Their chance to be like other people. If they did well, and why mightn't they, with a vessel like that, they'd have, after a while, money to buy or build a regular house and get clothes of their own and the things they needed. It was a fresh start. And he and Emily both knew what a fresh start felt like.

Perhaps the Frasers wouldn't do well. There was always a chance they'd skip off sometime and sell the sloop and not come back. That was the risk Dad took, just as old Dale and young Dale had taken a risk on that ice cake. But Dad wasn't afraid of a risk.

Ken was proud to have had a share, even a small one, in building the new sloop, and Emily must have felt the same way, for she looked across the table at him, her pretty two-colored eyes very serious, and said in a low voice, "I helped put on the gold leaf."

Just then Mother Philbrook went to the stove and came back with the coffee pot.

"Another cup all round," she said cheerfully. "And let's wish the Frasers happiness and success."